WELCOME
DEEP CR...

KELLY—She's there to b... ...es, but she can't help bein... ...d that Jeff Mitchell has signed up too.

JEFF—Just the thought of being around Kelly with the dancing green eyes almost drives Jeff crazy, but he can't let anything get in the way of his admittance to Harvard.

BRIAN—Kelly has been his best pal forever . . . but his relationship with Paula is of a very different kind.

PAULA—Brian is her whole life, and she jealously clings to him wherever they go.

CHRIS—A lonely jock with a hot temper and severe mood swings, football is his obsession—to make up for all he doesn't have.

NATHAN—Hostile and sullen, he's at odds with Chris . . . and now he's got something on him.

ISABEL—She carries the knife that belonged to her Indian grandfather . . . just to protect herself.

ANGEL—Dressed in black, her hair spiked, she speaks in strange ways . . . and warns of the danger of the lake.

Crash Course

NICOLE DAVIDSON

AN AVON  FLARE BOOK

AVON BOOKS
A division of
The Hearst Corporation
105 Madison Avenue
New York, New York 10016

Copyright © 1990 by Kathryn Jensen
Published by arrangement with the author
Library of Congress Catalog Card Number: 89-92495
ISBN: 0-380-75964-0
RL: 6.2

First Avon Flare Printing: July 1990

AVON FLARE TRADEMARK REG. U.S. PAT. OFF. AND IN OTHER COUNTRIES,
MARCA REGISTRADA, HECHO EN U.S.A.

Printed in the U.S.A.

RA 10 9 8 7 6 5 4 3 2 1

FOR DAVE,
the best one-armed wrestler
at OMHS

Prologue

A devilish night wind shifted the tree branches high overhead—rustling pine needles, sending tiny, razor-sharp twigs down the collar of his varsity jacket. Ignoring them the boy pushed the rowboat off the silty embankment and into the lapping wavelets of the black lake.

"Get in," he ordered.

The figure standing beside him in the middle of the woods shivered, but didn't move toward the boat.

"Get in," he repeated, more firmly. "There's no reason to put this off any longer."

Slowly, the figure obeyed, then sat down in the stern with a stiff jerk.

The boy went back for the Coleman lantern and stepped in too, gripping the gunwale as the rickety vessel dipped and wobbled in the shallows, splashing cold water against his already numb hand and wrist. He set the lantern on the floor between his passenger's feet and his own. Without another word, he slammed the oars into the oarlocks and began rowing with nervous energy.

The chill air nibbled at the ends of his already taut nerves, making it hard for him to concentrate on his strokes or his next, dreaded, move. Then reassuring words slid through his mind—like a Coke promo flashing across the electronic scoreboard in the end zone of Thomaston High's football field—*I'm seventeen years old. It's not like I'm gonna die or anything!* Just as important to remember was his reason for being here: he had to protect *her*, save her from this madness.

What had that dippy old Indian legend said?

Look into my black waters. You can see to the bottom of your soul . . . and there lies your fate.

What a load of crap! Yet . . .

The sky was overcast, no stars, no moon. Only the lantern's flickering glow for light. For the first time since they'd pushed off from shore, he dared to twist away from his passenger, and leaned to one side, glancing over his shoulder into the lake. A dim, orange reflection of his young face appeared in the instant before his oar slashed through the dark water.

A definite load of crap. Nevertheless, he sensed a greedy tug from the lake's depths—or from somewhere close by.

Straightening up sharply, he studied the shadowy form in the boat's stern. An hour ago, that expressive mouth had curled in menacing anger, spat out bitter accusations. Now, he could sense a change of mood. Fear seeped across the cold, reedy-smelling air. Good. Fear was what he'd hoped for, what he'd counted on to save them. But he clenched his teeth and rowed on, still unwilling to stop what he'd begun.

The boy pulled again and again on the oars, until the little wooden boat floated over what he and his friends, waiting back at the cabin, knew to be the deepest, most treacherous water.

Carefully he secured the oars, then stood up, bracing the soles of his sneakers on opposite sides of the hull for stability.

His throat tightened painfully. When he opened his mouth, a raspy voice came out that sounded as if it belonged to someone else. "Don't struggle. Just let the current pull you down. Soon as you're completely submerged, try to take a deep breath," he suggested, not unkindly. "The water will fill your lungs. It will be faster that way." Smiling crookedly, he took a step forward and reached out.

The one reaction he hadn't anticipated took him by surprise. The shadow in the stern sprang straight at him.

"No! No, I won't do it!" the mouth shrieked, inches from his own. Long fingers clawed at his jacket with shocking strength, ripping off the large felt letter T over his heart.

He lost his balance, staggered.

"Watch out!" he cried. "Oh, God, I didn't mean it!"

The boat rocked violently, and his right foot slipped on the scummy wood floorboards as the Coleman fell over and its flame sputtered out. For a fraction of a second, he pictured himself crashing down on the bench where he'd sat, breaking an arm or something. Instead, his body hit freezing water.

"Help me!" he cried once, before the wet weight of his heavy winter clothes and boots dragged him down. His gaping mouth filled with vile-tasting wa-

3

ter. The unwieldy shapes in his pockets rapidly pulled him further down through silky-cool layers.

Everything had happened so quickly, he hadn't managed to draw a full breath before the water closed over his head. He struggled to gain a few inches toward the surface, but without air—and after the exertion of rowing—he felt incredibly weak, incapable of keeping up the fight.

For a moment, he imagined he felt a hand grasping his jacket—pushing him deeper, or pulling him upward. The water during the day had been murky. At night, without the lantern above as a beacon, it was impossible to see through. He could no longer tell which way was up! Then the connection was broken. The hand, or whatever it had been, released him. And even as he thrashed his arms and legs in the irrational hope he might break the surface, his chest tightened, burning so agonizingly he was sure it would burst.

Too soon, a paralyzing lightness overtook him. He gave up to the water as the icy current from the spring below pulled him deeper . . . deeper. With a twinge of regret, he realized he'd never, never see her again.

Chapter 1

Kelly Peterson tossed her books and purse on the coffee table. Still clutching her keys, she ran back outside and down the block to the cluster of neighborhood mailboxes.

Ever since she'd been a little kid, Kelly had gotten excited about the mail. You just never knew what fantastic surprise might be waiting inside an envelope or package with your name on it. Today she'd pulled an A on a French test, the sun was shining, and a crisp November breeze was sweeping across the Baltimore suburb of Thomaston, scattering gray clouds that never produced any rain—all fine omens. Less than a week short of Thanksgiving vacation, this particular day had already been nearly perfect. There was bound to be something wonderful in the mail!

As soon as Kelly peered inside the tiny, dark cubicle, she changed her mind.

Frowning, she pulled out the only item inside, a large manila envelope marked TO THE PARENTS OF KELLY ANN PETERSON.

To the parents of . . . The curse of any high school student. But, to Kelly, the words had an especially traumatic ring, and a chill slid down her spine as she mentally corrected the address: *Not to the parents . . . to the father of Kelly Ann Peterson.*

Her eyes filled up and began to sting as she trudged slowly back toward the house. "Oh, hell," she muttered.

For the past two years, Kelly and her dad had been on their own. If her mother had been taken away from them by a fatal illness, or a car accident, even if she'd unwittingly walked into the cross fire of a gang fight in nearby Washington, D.C., which wasn't unheard of these days, Kelly figured she'd have been able to cope a little better than she had. Terrible, unfair things happened in the world. Hijackings, plastic explosives in airliners, kidnappings, earthquakes, nuclear plant disasters, mass murders—sometimes the fact that anyone at all was still alive on the planet seemed a miracle. But why did someone just walk away from the people who loved her?

Blinking her eyes dry, she sat down on the cement steps leading to the front door of her tidy, three-bedroom brick house. She stared at the envelope.

"Do I open you, or what?" she asked it. Even though her mood was considerably dimmer, her curiosity about the contents of the envelope continued to taunt her.

Considering the alternatives to outright mail tampering, Kelly held the envelope up to the brilliant sunlight. Nothing. Not even a shadow. She shook it. Couldn't tell anything that way, dammit! On an impulse, she locked the front door and jogged off down the street, taking her father's mail with her.

She hadn't had a good long chat with her old friend

6

Brian Lopez in quite a while. Since he worked fourth period in the admin office as an aide, he might know what was in the envelope.

A few minutes later, the glitzy new condo complex at the foot of the hill loomed in front of her. She turned in at the first gravel drive, ran up the sidewalk, and rang the Lopez's bell—an ornate brass knob that twisted, setting off chimes somewhere deep inside.

Waiting impatiently for a response, she glanced into the beveled glass panes alongside the door. Her reflection revealed a tangle of shoulder-length red curls, flushed cheeks that normally were a clear ivory, and wide-set green eyes. She practiced a grin. Teeth— glorious, straight, white teeth—framed in a great smile. They were her pride. Four lousy years of braces, but it had been worth it. Without a trace of ego, she admitted she really had grown into herself. She was pretty. At least pretty. Beyond that, she couldn't really say.

"What's with you, Bri?" she muttered, ringing a second time.

She pressed her ear to the door, listening. There definitely were voices coming from inside. Although muffled, they were raised in some kind of emotion. Maybe she should just discreetly leave, telephone later.

The door swung open.

"Kelly!" It was Paula Schultz, Brian's girlfriend.

Paula, a soft-spoken, petite blonde with enormous blue eyes and a heart of gold, was forever feeding stray cats or rescuing injured birds and other little, wild creatures. Her garage was a menagerie of rusting bird cages and dusty plastic Habitrails she'd begged off her friends, in which she housed her patients during their recoveries. More than anything, Paula wanted to become a veterinarian. But, even though Kelly admired Paula, they'd never become close. Paula was a very private person, with few friends, whereas Kelly never seemed to get serious with anyone and just enjoyed being included in a group.

"Oh, hi," Kelly said. "I'm not interrupting anything, am I?"

Paula frowned. "No, why would you think that?"

"Oh, I don't know. Brian's parents aren't here, are they? If my boyfriend and I—that is, if I *had* a boyfriend—anyway, if we were alone in my house, I'd like to think an unexpected visitor would be interrupting *something!*" Kelly bounced past Paula, into the marble-and-glass foyer. "Where's Brian?"

"In the den. But, we were sort of in the middle of a discuss—"

"That's okay . . . only be a minute." Kelly grinned reassuringly at Paula. She was so possessive. Another girl couldn't even look at Brian without Paula adding her name to a mental blacklist.

Skirting Paula, Kelly strode into the den that was as large as the whole first floor of her own house. Equipped with Ping-Pong and pool tables, a bar complete with every liquid refreshment known to mankind, wide-screen TV with VCR, pit-style sofa, and lots of cushy floor pillows—and still leaving plenty of room for dancing—this room had been the setting for many of their neighborhood parties.

"Hi, Bri!" she called out brightly when she saw

him stretched out on one section of white leather couch.

He sat up quickly, smiling so broadly she knew he was genuinely glad to see her. "Kelly! Hey, what's up?"

"Well . . ." She plopped down on a convenient floor cushion and played with the envelope flap, contemplating how an inch of loose edge she'd just now discovered might respond to a little steam. "You work as an admin aide. I was just wondering if there had been a bulk mailing to parents in the last week. You know, PTA stuff or anything."

"No. Nothing that I can think of," Brian answered.

Just what she'd been afraid of. If it wasn't routine stuff, it *must* be bad news of some sort, though she couldn't imagine what. She'd kept her grades up since September and even had a shot at making first-semester honors.

"That's too bad," she murmured. "A letter to my father came in today's mail from the school. He's been so tense lately about his work, I was hoping to find out what it's about. If it's bad news, I'd like to break it to him gently."

"That's very considerate," said Brian.

"And, if it's *really* bad news, I'm seriously considering torching it."

"Kelly!" Paula let out a strange, forced laugh. "You know you wouldn't."

For the first time, Kelly noticed that Paula's eyes looked red, as if she'd been crying. She suspected that the two of them had been arguing again about

9

their future. They'd been going together for as long as anyone could remember. Since their freshman year, Kelly guessed, thinking back. Now they were all juniors. Remaining an item for more than a year was an eternity for anyone in the social whirl at Thomaston. But Brian and Paula seemed to be made for each other.

In fact, Brian was much like Paula in many ways: light-complexioned, despite his father's Hispanic genes, sensitive, smart. His dad had been a colonel in the air force before he retired to start his own real estate business in Thomaston. Lopez Realty had skyrocketed the family into the realm of comfortable wealth. Brian had the grades and the money to go to any Ivy League school, but an early appointment from Senator Delaney to the Air Force Academy in Colorado had been a dream come true for him—until it created a major problem for him with Paula.

Paula's parents refused to let her go as far away as Colorado for college, and ever since Brian had gotten his appointment, she'd been begging him to turn it down so they could attend college together closer to home. Brian usually gave in to Paula, but on this he was holding firm. But Kelly was certain they'd work things out. They were so obviously in love and wanted to be together. Kelly wished she had someone she felt that strongly about—and who felt that way about her.

Paula coughed lightly, as if trying to hurry things along. "You know, my folks received something from the school yesterday."

"Why didn't you say so?" Kelly choked out.

"I didn't think of it. I mean, I'd assumed that nobody else I knew would be going on Mr. Porter's retreat. Then Brian signed up for it, and—''

''*That's* what this is about?'' Kelly gasped. ''The SAT crash course Porter is hosting over Thanksgiving vacation?''

''Is that the envelope?'' Brian asked, pointing to the distinctive yellow rectangle in her hand.

''Yeah.''

''That's it. Mine came today too.''

Kelly groaned, collapsing onto the floor. ''I can't believe he'd do this to me! My own father. Five days! He expects me to spend all five days of my Thanksgiving vacation holed up in some hick cabin in the woods studying for SATs? *Nobody* studies for SATs!''

''Sorry, old girl,'' Brian said softly.

''Look, I don't know about you two, but I'm getting out of this slave-labor camp. No way am I going to let anyone rob *me* of my hard-earned vacation.''

Kelly had been working her tail off since September, determined to make her junior grades impressive enough to withstand the closest scrutiny of any scholarship committee. That way she wouldn't have to attend the local community college—which was, in everyone's estimation, the pits. Funds in her family, unlike those of the Lopez clan, were not unlimited. And she had absolutely no desire to join the military.

Kelly popped up onto her feet.

''What are you going to do?'' Brian asked.

''Call my dad at work.'' She started for the door.

''Isn't it almost time for him to leave?'' Brian asked.

''Yeah.''

11

"Well, use our phone. There's one behind the bar, on the wall."

Paula shot him a testy look.

The bitch, thought Kelly, *she can't even let his best and oldest friend spend ten minutes in the same room!* Feeling as if she were intruding, Kelly dialed hurriedly, then waited for someone to pick up.

"Yes, hello," she said politely when a syrupy voice answered at the Department of Energy, extension 158. "Is Frank Peterson at his desk?"

God, am I tired, Kelly thought as she waited. *What could have possibly possessed the man to do this?*

On top of her schoolwork, there had been her drama class's fall musical, *Cats.* Their director had received special permission to use the popular script and score, since proceeds were going to Children's Hospital in Washington. She'd played Grizabella, which was a wonderful part, and she loved performing. But keeping up with her homework while attending the endless rehearsals, which had begun even before the end of summer, had exhausted her. She needed a rest. She *deserved* a rest!

Then a terrible thought struck her. She hung up.

"What's wrong?" Brian asked.

"I'd better wait until he comes home. It just occurred to me—he probably signed me up hoping to make Thanksgiving easier on both of us. Holidays, the last two years, have been pretty rough," she admitted.

"So," Paula asked, as if trying to sound indifferent, "are you going to go to Deep Creek?"

Kelly shrugged. "I don't know. Last Thanksgiving

was pretty gross. But spending this one slaving over practice tests would be hell.''

As it turned out, Kelly didn't know the half of it.

Jeff Mitchell left his last class of the day thirty minutes before the final bell, with the help of an early dismissal note from his mother—which *he* had very carefully written.

He drove his white Corvette ZR-1 over to the teachers' lot at the west entrance to the school and sat with the motor idling, drumming his fingers impatiently on the leather-wrapped steering wheel while he waited.

His parents had wanted to buy him a BMW or a Volvo. Something substantial, quality, sensible. In short, a tank. But ever since Jeff had read *Car and Driver*'s review of the ZR-1, ''the Corvette from Hell,'' he'd hungered for its sweet 32-valve, 5.7-liter port-fuel-injected V-8 engine and max 380 horsepower. Zero to sixty in 4.5 seconds didn't sound too shabby either. On his test drive, he'd taken it up to 150 and it felt as if it could do 175 easy. So what if it only got sixteen miles per gallon around town. He sizzled in it—white lightning!

''Where are you, jerk?'' He muttered between gritted teeth. ''Come on. Show your face.''

He'd heard that Alexander Porter, his sophomore-year American history teacher, always left early. The man didn't believe in staying after school to meet with students who failed to keep up with his lectures during class time.

''I'm paid to teach four periods, five days a week,''

he'd tell his incoming students, every September. "If you're in one of my classes, you'd better be here, on time, ready to take notes till your little pinkies drop off. Four hours a day is all I can tolerate of teenagers. I expect that sixty minutes of me will be more than enough for you!"

Porter didn't mince words.

Neither did he stand for any nonsense in his room. Rumor had it the man possessed a violent temper, although Jeff had never personally witnessed it. He had, however, experienced the Porter special—the stone-cold stare that pierced a luckless victim clear through to the heart. When trapped within its laser-like power, even the bravest trembled helplessly, unable to create a credible excuse for missed work or poor performance on a test.

During his year in Porter's class, Jeff had worked harder than he had for any other teacher. Perversely, it was the only course in his initial three years at Thomaston that he hadn't aced. It spoiled his chance of having a pristine 4.0 at graduation, but he considered himself fortunate. Others had fared much worse.

Through prudent planning, Jeff had arranged to get all of his required courses out of the way before his senior year. Next year, all he had to do was cover his ass, make sure his GPA stayed nice and high by way of suitably uncomplicated electives. Harvard would welcome him with open arms.

Brother, how wrong could I have been!

Jeff's glance swerved momentarily, away from the side door with its wired-glass inset. The colorful red-

and-gold jerseys of the varsity football team appeared on the field below the math wing.

He could see several of his friends, but they were all dwarfed by one impressive hulk—Chris Baxter. The defensive tackle's black face and hands shone with sweat, even in the cool autumn air. Baxter's shirt bulged at the shoulders, biceps, pecs—and he wasn't even wearing pads!

Jeff couldn't make out any details of the guy's face from this distance, but he was sure the dark eyes were small and ruthless. That's how they'd always appeared to him from the stands during a game. Man, mused Jeff, that's one scary dude.

Then his attention was snagged by a sudden motion.

Alexander Porter, carrying a leather valise, strode rapidly down the sidewalk toward the parking lot.

Jeff thumped the steering column in triumph. *Gotcha, you bastard!*

Quickly he turned off the ignition, shoved open the Vette's door, and loped over to the sidewalk.

Porter had been staring at the pavement while moving with a swift, purposeful stride. He appeared vaguely startled when he looked up to see Jeff blocking his path, but recovered quickly.

"Ah—Mitchell, isn't it?"

"Yes, sir."

"Something I can do for you, Mr. Mitchell?"

The guy was pushing forty, but he still had all his hair, was a good six feet tall, and looked to be in adequate shape. Nothing, Jeff reassured himself, I can't handle. Two years on JV wrestling and another with the varsity team at the 167-pound slot had built up his strength. Nevertheless, some of Jeff's former bravado dwindled away under Porter's icy gaze.

"As a matter of fact," he began warily, stopping to clear his throat, "I was just wondering, sir, why you chose to solicit my parents for your SAT preparatory course."

"Solicit?" asked Porter, staring at him.

"Yes, sir. I don't think it was fair, your singling me out. I mean . . . otherwise, how would they have known about it?"

"The same way the other students and their parents became aware of the Deep Creek retreat—by reading the board of education newsletter mailed to every family in the district."

"Oh. Guess I missed it," Jeff muttered, feeling suddenly foolish.

Porter glared at him, waiting. "You have something more to say?"

"I . . . I . . . no."

"Fine. I'll see you Wednesday the twenty-second, on the bus in front of the school at six forty-five A.M."

Jeff's throat went dry. He couldn't swallow, couldn't force a single word between his parched lips. Never, by any stretch of imagination, had he considered himself a timid person. Why was this one crummy teacher able to fluster him so easily?

Porter stepped around him, starting away.

As if taking on a will of its own, Jeff's hand shot out, actually brushing the history teacher's coat arm. "I don't think I need the course," Jeff croaked.

Porter halted, slowly turning to face him again, his

eyes cold, damning. "Your parents seem to think you do."

"I . . . I realize that. It's just that they're nervous about the college boards, you know how parents get. I'll do fine. I don't need coaching."

"What about the first two times you took the boards, Mitchell?"

Jeff drew in a sharp breath. He hadn't realized his mom and dad would turn over that kind of information to a stranger. He considered his SAT scores personal. Like his birth certificate—with the tiny, inked footprints—or the snapshots his mom had taken of him climbing out of the bathtub when he was three. That sort of stuff in the wrong hands could prove embarrassing!

"I, um . . . I froze. I'll do better this time . . . with the experience."

"I know," Porter said, his eyes suddenly so penetrating that Jeff felt compelled to drop his glance. "But you won't do as well on your own as you'll be able to after I've dug into your brain and uncrossed a few wires. Maybe three . . . four hundred points higher in your case—*no sweat.*"

Surprised, Jeff looked up to observe Porter's emotionless water-blue eyes. Was he trying to make a joke? Jeff could have almost sworn that he was, with that uncharacteristic choice of slang.

"You do *want* to be accepted by Harvard, don't you?" asked Porter.

"Of course I do. I'd never be satisfied going to school anywhere else! Every male on my father's side of the family for five generations has graduated from Harvard.''

''So?''

Jeff took a deep breath. ''All right, all right,'' he grumbled. ''So maybe it's worth five days of misery. I'll be there.''

''Fine.''

Jeff shifted his feet uneasily on the pavement. A couple of teachers passed by on their way to their cars. The sound of buses revving up in the distance drifted toward him. But Jeff was reluctant to move.

''Since I'm going, I was just sort of wondering,'' he ventured. ''Your letter said there would be eight students in the group, all staying in one cabin at the edge of Deep Creek Lake. Could you tell me who else will be there?''

''That shouldn't matter, since you'll have precious little time to socialize, Mitchell.''

''Yeah, well—'' Jeff wanted reassurance he wouldn't be shacked up with seven complete dorks for the duration.

''I don't suppose it makes any difference,'' Porter said finally. He unclasped his briefcase and pulled out a sheet of paper. ''Here. I'd intended to post this, but the grapevine will probably work faster anyway.''

''Thanks.'' Jeff unconsciously started to breathe again, his eyes racing down the list of names even as Porter moved silently away from him.

Just before climbing into his car, the history teacher turned. For ten seconds Alexander Porter studied the tall, dark-haired junior through narrowed eyes. He was a smart boy, with an easygoing charm that had made him stand out from the general school population and encouraged others to listen to him, and follow.

This one could be trouble, he thought grimly, determining to keep an especially close eye on Jeff. He couldn't afford for anyone to get in the way of what he had to do.

Chapter 2

Except for some girl called Angel Manson, Jeff knew everyone on Porter's roster.

Angel. Pretty name.

He wondered idly if she had a face to match—or a body. She sounded a little like a stripper in a TV detective show. There was, however, another name that intrigued him far more: Kelly Peterson.

Three weeks ago, he hadn't known the effervescent redhead existed. For some reason, he'd just never focused on her as more than a frenzied orange blur in the corridor, and they'd never happened to share a class. Then he let himself get dragged along to the Friday performance of the school's musical.

"C'mon, Jeff," one of his closest friends, Warren Knight, had pleaded. "I want to see the show, and I'd feel like an idiot sitting alone."

Jeff winced. "I don't usually go for that sort of stuff. My kind of music is rock or nothing. I've heard the original cast recording of this show. My sister plays it in her bedroom. Over and over and over."

"Who cares about the music." Warren was beginning to sound desperate. He lowered his voice conspiratorially. "There's this girl—Sharon Lewis. She's got a minor role, but very major breasts. Follow me? I figure in a leotard she'll be spectacular!''

Jeff doubted that merely gawking at any girl's figure from across an auditorium could hold his attention for an entire evening. Especially the kind of girl who'd appeal to Warren: the airhead variety. Prepared to be bored out of his skull, he grudgingly handed over his four bucks for a student ticket the night of the show and took a seat in the sixth row beside a salivating Warren. The curtain went up. Fifteen minutes later, Jeff was in love.

Kelly was awesome. She stepped onto the dark stage, and the whole auditorium seemed to light up again. Her shoulder-length red hair was teased into a wild mane around her gamine face. Adorable whiskers and kitten-freckles had been applied to her cheeks. She wore a dynamite, if somewhat scraggly, fur leotard. When she purred and arched her long back—*is that how she'd react if I touched her?*—he nearly passed out in his seat.

But she wasn't really trying to be seductive or even flirtatious. He could tell, by observing her gestures, her graceful leaps and miming, how hard she must have worked to perfect the ''catness'' of her movements. She was good, *really* good, at what she was doing. When she sang her solo, ''Memory,'' he thought he would die of sadness and joy in the same moment.

Now, he'd discovered that Kelly was going to Deep Creek. For five days, they'd be together in the same cabin. Five sublime, Kelly-available days for him to—

''Oh, no!'' he breathed, suddenly feeling torn.

Regrettably, Porter had made a valid point. Jeff *did* want to get into Harvard in a bad way. To swing it, he'd have to raise his SAT scores considerably. Kelly, within reach, cluttering his mind with her adorable smiles and mind-boggling curves, wasn't going to help.

Well, he thought philosophically, there was only one thing to do. He'd have to use a little willpower, just play it cool when he was around her during the retreat. Then, after all this was over, reminiscing about their experiences at Deep Creek would be the perfect excuse for striking up a conversation at school. From there who could say where it would lead!

Jeff suddenly felt very good about Thanksgiving. He turned the key in the Corvette's ignition and stepped on the gas.

Just as he was slowing down for the stop sign at the exit from the faculty lot, some idiot darted out in front of the car, frantically waving his hands above his head. Jeff jammed his foot on the brake. The Corvette skidded to a stop barely a foot in front of the guy's knees.

Shaking inside, Jeff hit a button on the dash. The driver's window slid down with a sweet hum. "What the hell are you doing, Grant?" he demanded. "I could have flattened you!"

Nathan Grant ran around to the side and leaned in the window. "Hey, man, I need a ride," he gasped. "How about it?"

He was a lanky kid who always wore a patched leather jacket, reflective sunglasses, and biker's boots. Not one of Jeff's crowd, or honor society material.

Jeff sighed, still under the effect of a mellow mood, Kelly on his mind. What the hell, he thought. "Where to?"

"Cinema Five."

"Hop in." He flicked the control on the dash that unlocked the passenger side and waited for Nathan. "Going to catch an early show?"

"Naw." Nathan chewed loudly on a wad of gum as he swung himself into the seat. "Work there. Sell tickets. Make popcorn. You know." Nathan seemed to favor two-word sentences, at least when talking to people he didn't know well.

"Now that you mention it," Jeff admitted, "I guess I have seen you there a couple times."

There was something else they shared, other than frequenting the Cinema Five. Nathan's name had been on Porter's list, and now it seemed funny to Jeff that they'd run into each other this way. After all, only eight people out of a population of nearly a thousand students was a pretty select group. Still, there was room in the world for coincidence. He assumed Nathan's motorcycle was out of commission. Pressed to get to work on time, the guy probably would have flagged down the first person he saw.

Jeff cleared his throat and steered into the flow of cars moving in a steady stream out of the student parking lot. "I understand we're going to be spending vacation together—well, doing the same thing anyway."

"You're kidding."

Jeff couldn't make out Nathan's eyes behind the silver lenses. It was impossible to tell from his tight smile what he might be thinking.

Jeff nodded toward his books on the floor behind his seat. "There's a paper with everyone's name who'll be at Deep Creek, if you want to take a look."

Nathan twisted around and extracted the list from between books. "Isabel Smith," he read in the monotone of someone who still has to concentrate on syllables, "Paula Schultz—she's that blonde chick, the varsity football cheerleader, right?" Jeff nodded. "Brian Lopez, you, me, Angel Manson—don't know him—"

"Him?" Jeff scowled. Well, that was possible, he guessed. If so, he was probably a biker like Nathan. From what little he knew of that breed, they favored strange names. "Must be from another school," he added vaguely.

"Right. Kelly Peterson," Nathan continued, without reacting to the name that sent shivers straight to Jeff's toes, "and—geez. This is too much, man. Count me out."

"Why? What's wrong?"

"Chris Baxter. He's coming."

"You prejudiced?"

"Hell no."

"Then you have something against jocks." Jeff, who ran on the cross-country team as well as wrestled, was tired of the bad rap athletes received at Thomaston, a school with mediocre teams even in their best years.

"Baxter's a monster!" Nathan whined. "You expect me to bunk with him?"

24

"I'm sure once you get to know him—"

"Oh, right. Some kid, he stuck out his hand to congratulate Baxter after a game. Instead of just shaking, Baxter crushed it. Broke ten bones."

"I heard that story too," Jeff admitted. "There had to be more to it."

"Hah!"

"Listen, it's not like you're going to be stranded out in the boonies alone with him. There are eight of us, plus Porter."

"Yeah, well . . ." Nathan muttered, his male ego, what there was of it, swinging into action. "I just wouldn't turn my back on him, if I were you."

Jeff drove for a while in silence. He was beginning to regret his generosity. Nathan was a strange sort: kept to himself a lot, wore shades year-round—even indoors. Probably did coke or something; that's why he hid his eyes.

Still, Jeff figured Thanksgiving would be far more pleasant if he got along with his cabin mates.

"Why are *you* sacrificing your vacation?" Jeff asked to break the silence when they were almost to the theater.

"My old man."

"He signed you up?"

"Naw. He gave the speech. I signed." Nathan shifted lower in his seat, scrunching his body to make it look as if he'd put on about thirty pounds. He belched, to add authenticity to his imitation. "Hey, punk. You's graduatin' next year. Better start lookin' for a real job, an' a pad a yer own. Free ride's gonna be over." Stretching out his long legs, Nathan grinned. "I don't want to spend the rest of my life making popcorn, or end up in a go-nowhere job like my old man, so I guess I better keep going to school."

Jeff swallowed as he took a left at the Cinema Five marquee. His parents would never treat him like that—just throw him out after graduation. He glanced along the seat at Nathan with new sympathy.

"That's tough," Jeff said quietly.

"Yeah, well. Life's a bitch, huh?" Nathan's left hand caressed the creamy white leather cushion beside his hip. "Nice wheels. This must have run you—what? Twenty . . . thirty grand?"

"More like fifty," Jeff admitted reluctantly.

"Nice, man. Real nice."

"Thanks," Jeff said cautiously. The last time a guy he'd thought was a friend admired something of his, his bicycle had been stolen the following day. Envy made people do rash things.

The night before the group was scheduled to leave for Deep Creek, Brian showed up, unannounced, at Kelly's front door.

"Need help packing?" he asked cheerfully.

"Not really," she admitted. "Porter's directions eliminate almost everything except a couple changes of clothes."

"And plenty of paper and pencils."

Kelly laughed, nodding. "Come in anyway. It's been a long time since we just hung out together." She glanced at him sideways. "You seem to be in an unusually good mood. Paula let you off for a few hours for good behavior?"

"She just depends on me," he explained, following Kelly upstairs to her bedroom. "Sometimes she overdoes it."

She wondered why he wasn't at *her* house, helping *her* pack. Maybe the bickering had just become too much for him. Sometimes she thought he'd be better off with someone else—someone who didn't suffocate him. But she'd never have suggested it. And he'd never have listened if she had.

Before long they were up in her room, chatting and joking, just like old times when they'd been in the seventh grade.

"You know," she said, after pulling nearly everything out of her closet, "I think it would be a lot easier if I just took everything. I can't make up my mind."

Brian sat in the middle of her bed, looking overwhelmed by the piles of sweaters, jeans, sweatshirts, and dresses around him. "Get real. Porter's rules say we're each allowed one suitcase or bag. This stuff could fill half a dozen steamer trunks!"

"I know. I know!" she wailed. "But there's a lot riding on my wardrobe for this trip."

A few hours after Kelly had plucked her father's letter from the mailbox, she'd received a call from a friend of a friend of a friend of none other than Jeff Mitchell—who'd told her that Jeff would be part of the Deep Creek group.

"I can't think straight!" Kelly cried in exasperation, tossing down an armload of assorted acid-faded, stone-washed, and virgin indigo jeans. "Let's go down to the kitchen for a cup of coffee."

27

"It's almost midnight. You sure it's all right with your dad if I stay this late?"

Kelly shrugged. "He's probably asleep in his room by now. I've been setting my own bedtime for years." Two, to be exact.

Kelly boiled water in the teapot. They made instant and used powdered creamer.

"What's the big deal about your clothes?" Brian asked, once they were seated at the kitchen table.

"You mean you didn't hear who's going to Deep Creek?"

He shook his head, taking a sip of coffee.

"Jeff Mitchell," she said, rolling her eyes.

Brian grinned. "Congratulations. How'd you swing that one?"

"I swear, I had nothing to do with it. Pure luck, that's all it is. Only, all of a sudden, I'm not so sure about spending five days with him in the woods."

"How come?"

"I don't know. The situation isn't exactly ideal."

"Oh, you'd rather spend five days stranded on a desert island with Mr. Hunk?"

Kelly laughed and nudged Brian playfully in the ribs. "Maybe. Maybe I would. At least then he wouldn't have any alternative female companionship."

"Come on, what are you worried about? I can't think of a girl at Thomaston who holds a light to you, Kell."

She grinned, glancing down into her cup. "Thanks," she murmured, touched by his loyalty. "But I'm not sure how gorgeous I'll be at the end of five days without a blow-dryer or curling iron. Remember rule number five? No electricity."

"Guess you'll have to depend upon your natural beauty," Brian said, a teasing glint in his eyes.

"Right. Red frizz and freckles. I'm sure Jeff will be bowled over."

"Don't forget, dress of the day—to quote Mr. P.'s letter—warm, loose, and casual."

Kelly groaned. "Translation: sweats or baggy jeans. *Very* provocative." She wrinkled her nose in distaste.

"So bring along a sexy negligee for those star-studded nights."

"Very funny. I'm not out to seduce the boy. I just want to get to know him better."

Of course, I might not object too strongly if he tried to kiss me . . . or something.

Brian looked at her solemnly, as if reading her thoughts. "Just don't get hurt, okay?" He took a deep breath, watching her intently, and she sensed that he was on the verge of saying something more. Finally, be blinked, and a closed expression fell over his soft, gold-and-olive eyes. Reaching over, he ruffled her rust-colored curls. "Look out for yourself."

She huffed. "Since when have I not?"

"Sorry," he said quietly. "You're a big girl now, huh?"

"Exactly."

"So, I should mind my own business. I'll pick you up at twenty till seven." He drained the remainder of his coffee in one gulp, then stood up from the table.

"You don't have to do that. I can drive myself.

29

Besides," she couldn't help teasing as she trailed behind him toward the door, "won't you have to clear it with Paula first?"

"No!" Brian snapped, coming to an abrupt stop. He spun to face her, his shoulders rigid, cheeks flushed.

His sudden anger took her by surprise. "Bri, I didn't mean . . ."

Almost immediately his expression softened and he shook off her apology. "Sorry, I shouldn't bite your head off like that. Of course Paula won't mind. But I just want you to know that, even if she did, I'd still come to get you. We'll always be friends. No matter what."

Kelly rose on tip toe and gave him a quick hug. "Exactly." For a moment, she rested her cheek on his firm chest, listening to the sound of his heart. Then she moved out from his arms, smiling. "I'd like to ride with you."

Brian touched the tip of her nose with one outstretched finger. "Remember to pack your minicorder."

" 'No tapes allowed,' " she cited the brochure. " 'Recorders to be used for scholastic purposes only.' "

Brian grinned. "See you, Kell."

From the rear seat of Brian's vintage '67 Mustang, Kelly surveyed the nearly-deserted parking lot of Thomaston High. She spotted Chris Baxter right away. In his bright blue UCLA sweatshirt, he was sort of hard to miss as he lounged against a shrunken version of the familiar yellow school bus.

Most of the guys at school were terrified of Chris and consequently granted him right of way in the halls. But he'd never bothered Kelly. In fact, when they were freshmen, he'd seemed a polite, average-sized guy with a bashful sense of humor.

Chris still said hello to her when their paths crossed. She often wondered what had happened in the last two years that had changed him so. Today, he looked lonely without his Tomcat teammates around him, swatting him congratulations on the ass, thumping his helmet. She felt sorry for him.

Then she saw *the girl,* and Kelly forgot all about the black football player. Porter's list had said her name was Angel something-or-other. Whoever she was, she wasn't a Thomaston student. This chick would have definitely stuck in her mind if she'd seen her before.

Angel wore her jet-black hair brutally straight, chopped off in jagged layers, with a few inky strands smoothed slickly around her cheekbones. Even from this distance, her eyes were enormous, dramatically outlined in kohl. Her loose, belted black dress hung limply over matching knit pants and black boots. Although she was without a coat, she didn't seem cold in the forty-degree wind that whipped around the corner of the school.

"Well, let's get this over with," Brian said from the front seat.

Paula glanced quickly at him, then away. "Is *she* going with us on the bus?"

Already checking out the competition, Kelly thought. "Looks that way. She is a bit . . . unusual, isn't she?"

"She seems . . ." Paula evidently had to search for a kind word too. ". . . slim."

Slim was an understatement. The girl was pale, gaunt, and appeared to have intentionally accentuated these traits with her morbid choice of clothing, makeup, and hairstyle.

Yanking her wheeled suitcase by its strap, Kelly started toward the bus. As she drew closer she kept one eye on Angel. Kelly noticed the other girl's fingernails were a full inch longer than her own—and painted black. Her lipstick, which had merely looked dark from a distance, was also black.

"Must be a real scream at a party," she muttered under her breath. She looked around anxiously. Jeff wasn't here yet, or Nathan Grant, one of the other boys she'd heard would be in their group.

"Hi," said a voice from close by.

Kelly spun around.

"I'm Isabel. Isabel Smith."

Smiling, Kelly dropped the strap to her bag and held out her hand. "Glad to meet you, Isabel. I'm Kelly Peterson. You're new at Thomaston, aren't you?"

"Yes," Isabel said. "We've just moved into town." She had a soft, sweet smile that was kind of exotic. Her eyes slanted subtly upwards at the outer edges, and her skin had a smooth, pale caramel glow, as if she'd been sunbathing recently. Kelly guessed Isabel might be part Hawaiian or Oriental.

32

"I saw you in my lit class. But I didn't get a chance to introduce myself," Kelly apologized.

"That's all right." Isabel looked around. "Is this it? Just the—one, two, three . . . Just the six of us?"

"If my sources are correct, two more are coming. Two guys."

Isabel grinned and Kelly realized with a jolt how really beautiful she was in a different sort of way. Her smooth, waist-length chestnut-brown hair spilled over her shoulders like a graceful waterfall. Her eyes were brown, wolflike in their motion and energy, darting constantly from person to person, seeming to absorb every detail, every movement around her. Yet there was also a gentleness in them that drew Kelly to the girl.

"Four girls, four guys," mused Isabel.

"I'm sure people won't be pairing off," Kelly said. "Porter will be keeping us too busy. We'll be lucky if he gives us time to eat and breathe."

Isabel glanced at the bus, her face serene. Porter had just appeared and was talking with the driver. "He'll give us time to be together," she said. "He's a very sensitive man."

"Huh?" Kelly gasped. "Are we talking about the same person?"

Slowly, Isabel turned back to face Kelly, her eyes confident. "Mr. Porter is a kind man who wants only to help us. What he does, he does because it will be best for us. He won't punish us for taking his course."

Kelly shrugged. "Whatever you say." Obviously Isabel didn't have Porter for a class.

A moment later, the teacher was waving them all

33

onto the bus. Nathan arrived, joining them after parking his beat-up Harley beside Brian's car. Chris Baxter had gotten on the bus first and taken the entire rear bench for himself. No one else chose a seat further back than halfway on the bus.

Kelly sat next to a window and looked out across the parking lot. Jeff still hadn't shown, and she was really beginning to worry.

"Do you think he's backed out?" she whispered.

Brian and Paula were seated directly behind her. "Relax," advised Brian. "He'll be here. You think Porter would let one of his victims escape that easily?"

"I suppose not," admitted Kelly. After hearing what her father had paid for these five days, she'd taken a very skeptical view toward their honorable teacher. Unless he planned to feed them lobster and filet mignon every day, he'd be making a hefty profit for less than a week's work.

The driver started the engine. Porter, still on the sidewalk beside the bus, pacing, had just consulted his watch for the third time when the unmistakable sleek silhouette of a white Corvette turned in at the gate at the far end of the school driveway. The car sped toward them, screeching to a stop beside the bus.

Kelly tried not to stare as Jeff Mitchell stepped out from behind the wheel, his neatly trimmed brown hair mussed as if he'd only just dragged himself out of bed. He wore tight jeans, his red-and-gold wrestling jacket open in the front to reveal a dazzling white polo jersey.

Kelly let out a long, ragged breath. "Oh, my."

"Is this seat taken?" a voice asked, scattering her thoughts.

"What? Huh?" She looked up at Isabel.

"I was sitting by myself. I thought you might like some company too."

"Oh, um, well . . ." Kelly stammered. She wanted to scream: *No! Go away, you fool!* But honestly, what were the chances Jeff would choose to sit beside her, a total stranger, when there were all these empty seats? "Sure," she said with a quick smile, patting the cushion beside her. "Why not."

Isabel shoved a small overnight bag under the seat in front of them and sat down. "How long is the ride to Deep Creek?" she asked brightly.

"Three hours."

"Good, then we'll have plenty of time to get acquainted. Tell me a little about yourself.

Kelly glanced out the window. Jeff was no longer in sight. Probably Porter was chewing him out for being late.

"Why don't you go first," Kelly suggested absently.

"Okay." Isabel launched into an animated soliloquy on her favorite foods, movies, books, and interests, leaving Kelly free to nod periodically.

Kelly watched the front of the bus, anticipating Jeff's entrance. Angel sat on the very front right-hand seat, her shoulder blades pressed up against the window, her legs stretched out along the seat so that her pointed black boots stuck out into the aisle. The girl intrigued Kelly. She rummaged through a velvet drawstring pouch, took out a peach, and bit into it hungrily.

Almost immediately, the driver turned around. "No food on the bus," he commanded.

Angel regarded him blankly and bit again.

"I said, no food, missy. I'm not gonna be cleaning up you kids' garbage. Tomorrow's a holiday."

Mr. Porter came up the stairs, followed by Jeff, who carried a soft-sided suitcase. The tall wrestler did a double take when he first saw Angel, tripped over his own feet, then, recovering his balance, dropped into a seat not far from the front.

Kelly covered her mouth with one hand to stifle a giggle.

The driver turned to Porter. "Tell that kid she can't be eatin' on my bus."

The history teacher took a second to sum up the situation. Then he faced Angel, his jaw tight, eyes frosting over.

The bus fell silent, waiting for first blood.

"Put the fruit away until we reach Deep Creek." Porter's voice was low, barely audible from where Kelly sat in the middle of the bus. Nevertheless, it sent a shudder through her.

But Angel stared up at Porter from her semi-reclining pose, her face expressionless except for a subtle glitter in her black eyes.

"Put . . . it . . . away!" he repeated, barely containing his anger.

Brian leaned over the top of the seat and whispered in Kelly's ear, "What a match. They're giving each other the evil eye."

36

"My money's on him," Kelly murmured.

But even now she was unable to keep her eyes off Jeff. She glanced diagonally across the aisle at him, stirred anew by his marvelous profile—strong, square chin and masculine nose. How depressing, she thought, he hadn't even looked back at her once since he'd come on board the bus. Kelly followed the probable direction of his eyes, to Angel.

As tense seconds ticked past, Porter glared at the strange girl, who, unbelievably, didn't so much as flinch. Then, in a move that was sure to grab everyone's attention—if they hadn't already been spellbound by the confrontation—Angel held the partially eaten peach high in one hand. Slowly, she closed her fingers over it, squeezing until her knuckles turned white.

Juice glistened between her fingers, running down her thin bare wrist and arm. In a flash, she thrust the mangled yellow flesh between her lips—and swallowed.

"Gross!" Nathan cried, a note of awe in his voice.

"She swallowed it, pit and all," whispered Paula.

Kelly shook her head. "All bets are off, Bri."

With an air of triumph, Angel gazed up at Porter, her chin dripping, eyes gleaming.

For a moment, he looked vaguely confused. Then he turned with a jerk, sat in the seat behind the driver, and ordered gruffly, "Drive!"

Kelly decided, right then and there, that the next five days would undoubtedly be the weirdest of her life.

* * *

The bus turned onto Route 70, then headed due west through the rolling Maryland countryside. The fields lay dead and brown under a gray November sky.

An hour later, Isabel had extracted every bit of personal information Kelly was willing to divulge and was now pumping Paula for her life story. The heater was turned up too high; the air was stuffy. A hypnotic drone from the engine lulled Kelly toward sleep. At last, she gave in to the pleasant drowsiness, rolled her jacket into a pillow, and propped it against the frosty window to cushion her cheek.

She dreamt.

At first, it was a wonderful dream—about Jeff and her. They held hands, walking through a lush, sun-speckled forest, gazing into each other's eyes. The air was softly warm. Furry little creatures scuffled through the undergrowth, peeking out now and then, or tumbling over each other as if to entertain the young couple.

Delighted, Kelly laughed at their antics. Jeff too seemed to be enjoying them. But his attention was more firmly focused on her. She could feel the intensity of his eyes.

"I love you, Kelly," he murmured in her ear.

With an expectant smile she turned to face him. But he was gone. In his place stood a figure wearing a mask . . . a wolf mask . . . eyes glowing.

"Come with me." the creature invited, and she couldn't tell if it was still Jeff's voice or another's, a man or a woman's. "Come deeper, into the woods with me."

She dug in her heels, stiffening, trying to pull free of the grip that had suddenly moved upward and become painfully tight on her arm.

Paula appeared at her side. "It's all right," she encouraged her. "He's an innocent little animal. See, his paw is hurt."

Kelly looked down at her arm again. Instead of fingers restraining her, sharp claws curled around her wrist. She cringed, pulling away. The claws slipped off her arm but, in doing so, slashed her flesh. Blood dripped on the ground. *Her* blood! Accumulating at her feet in a shiny red puddle. And she couldn't understand why she wasn't running away, fleeing for her life!

"You must trust him," Paula pleaded. "He trusts you. Wherever he goes, you must follow."

"No!" screamed Kelly. "No!"

Paula shook her head sadly. "You don't understand him, Kelly. Not like I do." And she put her arm around the wolf, leading him off into the dense brush.

Moments later, shrieks of terror and the agonized baying of a wild creature awoke Kelly with a start.

Chapter 3

"What's wrong? Are you all right?" a worried voice asked.

Kelly blinked, sitting up straight on the hard bus seat. Sweat ran down her trembling upper lip. She wiped it away with the back of her hand, staring at Isabel. "I . . . I fell asleep. A dream."

"Must have been a whopper."

Kelly nodded, squeezing her eyes shut and opening them, again and again. The wolf had seemed so threatening, so vivid, like something contrived by a Hollywood special-effects expert for a horror film. Yet, in the way of dreams, he was familiar. As if, in another persona, she passed him in the hallways at school every day.

Isabel leaned in front of her to peer out the window, gripping the steel frame for support. On the middle finger of her left hand was a ring. Still fighting off the chilling effects of her dream, Kelly concentrated on Isabel's jewelry. Actually, it was one of the most beautiful rings she had ever seen—silver, in the shape of a sunburst, with a polished turquoise center. She was about to comment on it, when a loud, rattling noise erupted from the rear of the bus. Both girls turned.

Chris Baxter, his face pressed against the rear window, wide nose squashed to one side, snored again. This time he sounded more like a growling grizzly bear.

"Poor Chris," Kelly murmured, wondering if his snore had somehow been transposed into her dream as a snarl.

"You know him?" Isabel asked, her eyes bright with curiosity.

Paula leaned forward from the seat behind. "Everyone knows Baxter. If you're smart, you'll steer clear. He's bad news."

Isabel considered the semi-prone, muscular hulk. "I think he's kind of . . . cute."

Paula hooted.

"What's going on?" Brian asked.

"She thinks Chris B. is *cute*. That's a first."

Kelly shifted awkwardly on her seat. "Don't put him down, Paula. He's not so bad."

"With those gross muscles and a neck like a sequoia?" Paula whispered, as if afraid Chris might hear.

Kelly glanced at Brian. Out of loyalty, Paula had to at least pretend Chris's type of build didn't turn her on, although she—along with the rest of the Thomaston cheerleaders—went wild every time he smashed through an opposing team's line.

"I don't know," Isabel said thoughtfully, a bashful smile lifting the corners of her mouth, "I kind of like muscles on a man."

"Talk to the woman," Brian ordered, looking

41

meaningfully at Kelly. He settled back in his own seat with Paula.

Obviously disappointed, Isabel frowned. "What's wrong with Chris?"

"Nothing," Kelly said. "He's just got this attitude. Chris has always been nice to me, but when he gets really steamed . . ." She shook her head, adding hastily, "I don't believe he's ever intentionally hurt anyone."

Isabel cast a last thoughtful glance over her shoulder in sync with another thunderous snore.

The bus left the highway, turning north. Before long, they were on a two-lane local route with low, forested mountains all around them. The driver ground gears, downshifting to take a hill into a valley. Houses appeared farther and farther apart until at last there were only occasional dirt paths leading away from the road and an infrequent cottage or boat rental shop, its windows boarded up. They passed a car headed in the other direction only twice during the next twenty minutes. Living midway between two sizable cities, Baltimore and Washington, D.C., Kelly had forgotten this sort of isolation existed only three hours away from home.

"Hey, man, how much longer we got to go?" Nathan called out.

Porter had been making notes in a loose-leaf binder. Turning, he viewed Nathan over the gold rims of his glasses. "Fifteen minutes." He closed the notebook and stood. "We might as well use the last leg of the journey for a briefing session. Somebody wake up Baxter so he won't miss this."

42

No one moved.

"Lopez, you."

Brian cleared his throat as if something had suddenly clogged it. "Um, sir. I'd really rather not."

"Why the hell—Oh, never mind. Mr. Mitchell, if you please."

Kelly couldn't help smiling as she observed Jeff's surprise, then the predictable hesitation. He'd probably prefer wrestling a ravenous crocodile than be the one to wake Chris "the Madman" Baxter out of a sound slumber.

"It's all right," Kelly said quickly, to save him embarrassment. "I'll do it."

She stepped over Isabel's knees. Grasping seat backs to brace herself against the bus's erratic jounces, she staggered toward the rear. Every eye, including the two sexy blue ones belonging to Jeff, was fixed on her, and she was delighted to have lucked into a way of getting herself noticed.

Kelly had the technique down pat. Her father woke roughly. "Like a soldier," he'd once called the habit, instantly alert, convinced of impending danger.

Gauging the stretch of Chris's near arm, she planted her feet as far from him as possible and reached out. At her first tap, his eyes flew open and, perhaps, seeing only her shadow, he lashed out wildly. Even with her precautions, she had to dance backward to avoid the powerful fist.

"Chris, it's okay! It's just me, Kelly."

"Huh? Wha—"

"We're almost to Deep Creek," she said gently. "You have to wake up now."

43

His eyes gradually focused on her, took in her smile. He gave her back a groggy smile and shoved himself upright. "Oh, sure. Sure, I'm up now."

"Good," she said. Then as an afterthought she added, "Glad you're with us, Chris."

He just grunted. But she felt certain it was a pleased grunt.

"Now then," Porter said, "a few rules. First of all, as you know we'll all be bunking in one cabin. It's plenty large, so we should have no trouble accommodating everyone comfortably. Girls will take one bedroom, boys a second, and I have the third. The central lounge area will serve as our classroom, kitchen, and dining hall. Any questions so far?"

"Is there only one bathroom for all of us to share?" Paula asked, glancing at Angel.

"There is *no* bathroom. The outhouse is behind the cabin."

"Outhouse?" Kelly squeaked.

"Whassa matter, Miss Priss?" taunted Nathan. "Got something against roughing it? What will I ever do without my bubble bath?" he squeaked out in a bad female impersonation.

Kelly glowered at him. "Sleazoid."

Nathan laughed.

Angel looked at Nathan with interest.

Oh, my, this is going to be the longest five days of my entire life, Kelly thought.

Then Jeff turned on his seat and gazed straight at her in a way that made blood rush into her cheeks, and she was suddenly dizzy, helpless, and didn't care if they were gone five months!

"Actually," she said, "I think it will be kind of fun, doing without luxuries for a few days."

Men weren't attracted to women who were too fussy. Kelly remembered reading that somewhere, probably in a *Cosmo* sexuality quiz. She loved taking those things, always scored high—which was reassuring, because she was still a virgin. It was good to know that apparently she had fantastic potential.

"Do we get to bathe in the lake?" she asked.

Jeff had been watching her but, now, abruptly turned away.

"If you can stand freezing water," said Porter, "you're welcome to plunge in the lake. The truth is, it's almost unbearably cold even during the summer. Especially out in the center, which you should stay away from anyway. The gentleman who rented this place to me warned about a tricky current out in the middle—something to do with the warmer water mixing with a cold spring from underground. Now—" He cleared his throat, ready to get down to business. "As soon as we arrive, everyone is to choose a bunk and stow his or her luggage beneath it. Make up your bed. If you need to use the facilities, you will take a buddy of the same sex with you."

A buddy? Kelly nearly laughed out loud. *What does he think we are, a Cub Scout troop?*

Porter's eyes had shrunk to intense dots, bright behind his glasses. "No one is to wander alone out of sight of the cabin, for any reason. And I don't want any boy-girl pairs disappearing into the woods without a third party *staying with them at all times.* Understood, Mr. Lopez? Miss Schultz?"

45

Brian and Paula nodded nonchalantly, as if they were accustomed to being singled out by teachers, field trip chaperones, and parents for similar precautions.

"And that goes for any other couples that may develop during the next few days." Porter's steady glare took in every face.

Kelly felt herself starting to blush. Could the man read her mind?

Isabel whispered, "Your boyfriend is here?"

"No," Kelly hissed, afraid Jeff would hear her.

"Maybe that's just as well . . . for you."

"What does that mean?"

Isabel shrugged and gave her a sad, wise look from far down in her brown eyes, but said nothing more. It occurred to Kelly that something was troubling her. Odd, she hadn't seemed to have anything on her mind when they'd first met in the parking lot a few hours earlier.

Did I miss something while I was asleep? Kelly wondered. But before she could put her concern into words the bus turned onto a dirt lane, bumping and wheezing through lofty pines, until they reached a barrier of fallen trees. Altogether, they must have come several miles from the main road.

"We'll go the rest of the way on foot," Porter announced, standing up.

"Man, this is massively wild!" Nathan hefted a torn canvas duffel bag onto one shoulder. "How far to our nearest neighbor?"

"Ten miles," Porter stated flatly. "During the summer most of the cabins around this end of the lake are occupied. In the fall, no one has much reason for being here."

"Except us gullible city folk," Jeff muttered behind Porter's back, just loud enough for the other students to hear.

Smiling, Kelly followed Jeff down the bus steps and looked around. The absolute silence was eerie. Trees seemed to soar a mile overhead, blocking out most of the sunlight. The undergrowth was dense and twisted, and Kelly immediately thought of snakes.

Shuddering, she turned to Isabel as the other girl hopped down beside her. "It could be days before anyone found a person who got lost out here."

"I can think of a pleasant way to spend a few days with you, sweet thing." Nathan proposed, leering at Kelly.

"Oh, please," she moaned.

He looked crushed, but only for a moment. "I'm here if you change your mind. In fact—" He raised his voice. "I'm here for anyone of the opposite sex in need of male companionship!"

No one rushed to take him up on his offer.

Once they were all off the bus, the driver checked for belongings left under the seats. "I'll be back on Sunday at noon," he told Porter.

"We'll be right here to meet you."

"If you decide to stay longer, just give me a call by Saturday."

Porter shook his head. "That won't be possible. There is no phone in the cabin, or anywhere around for miles."

"Ten," Nathan put in helpfully.

47

"Anyway," Porter added, eyeing Nathan grimly, "I'll be finished with them by then."

Not "We'll be ready for you," but *"I'll be finished."* As if he were polishing off a good meal of student brains, Kelly thought wryly.

"The cabin's another half a mile up this way," Porter continued as he led the group away from the bus. "Stay together. Follow directly behind me."

"Are there wild animals out here?" Angel asked, sounding hopeful.

"Very possibly, though I couldn't tell you what kind. I'm not much of an outdoorsman."

"Oh, swell," Jeff muttered.

Kelly grinned. Not only was he adorable, he had a sense of humor too.

"What was that, Mitchell?" demanded Porter, nudging his glasses up the bridge of his narrow nose, nearly tripping over a root in the process.

"I asked, 'Is there a well?' You know—for drinking water."

"Excellent question. No, there's no well. We'll boil lake water, although it's probably purer even without treatment than the stuff in most city reservoirs. However, there is another safety matter I should point out right away." He paused on the path, and his troops came to a halt, pretending to listen. "It's important that you stay on established paths, not go traipsing off into the woods, *and* watch for stones marked with red paint. This area is riddled with small caverns formed by underground springs. Most have dried up, but others still feed the lake."

"I heard about them when I was up here one year

48

with my dad," Paula said, looking around. "As the land erodes, it sometimes breaks through above a cavern."

"Correct." Porter gave her a coolly approving smile. "Park service employees take pains to mark those existing holes to prevent campers from stumbling into one. Just be careful where you step, we don't want any stubbed toes."

"Hell no," Nathan said with a straight face. "That would be tragic."

By the time they at last arrived at the cabin, everyone was short of breath and most of the kids were dragging their luggage. The building wasn't spectacular in any way. Weathered brown logs, cracks stuffed with gray clay. There was a charred spot in the middle of the clearing in front of the cabin's only exterior door, where earlier visitors had evidently built a fire. Between the trees, Kelly could make out a few strips of bleak November water.

Kelly chose the bunk directly beneath the only window in the girls' room. She unpacked a few of her cosmetics, the tiny teakwood box in which she kept a selection of earrings and bracelets, her brush and mirror, a large bottle of the sexiest perfume she could find—and set them along the rough wooden sill next to a photo of her father. The sheets were in the bottom of her suitcase, unfortunately, so she had to pull nearly everything out, then repack since there were no dressers. They'd also brought sleeping bags, in case the temperature continued to drop. Having completed her chores, she placed her favorite stuffed bear on her pillow and sat down on her bed to watch the other girls finish.

For the first time, she noticed Paula's bag—a compact carry-on satchel.

"Is that all you brought?" she asked.

Paula tucked her sheets over the mattress. "What do you expect with Porter's packing list?"

"You can't possibly have five changes of clothes in there."

"Well, I do," she snapped irritably. "I just know how to pack."

Since Paula didn't seem in the mood to chat, Kelly turned her attention to Isabel—who in her estimation was a far more interesting person anyway. "Want some help?"

"Sure. I think I'll take everything out of my suitcase. I can make neat piles under the bunk that will be easier to reach. Then I'll use my suitcase to collect dirty clothes."

"That's a good idea," Kelly said. Maybe she'd reorganize later too.

Kelly knelt on the floor beside the honey-skinned girl and began picking out T-shirts, already neatly folded, and stacking them. Talking to Isabel was easy, you just rode the surge of her chatter like a surfer who's caught a perfect wave. Whatever might have depressed the girl earlier must have been forgotten by now. Everything that came out of her pretty lips was upbeat, and she seemed interested in everyone in the group, eager to learn more about each of them. Kelly did her best to fill her in. She'd just reached into the

50

suitcase again when her fingertips touched something cold—and sharp.

"Ouch!" Kelly's hand snapped back on reflex.

"What's wrong?" Isabel asked, staring at the hairline gash on Kelly's finger that might have been a paper cut. A thin, red line of blood rose to the surface. "Oh, I'm sorry. I forgot—"

Isabel's hand disappeared for a moment beneath a sweater. When it came out again, a wicked silver blade nearly eight inches long lay across her palm.

"What's *that* for?" Kelly gasped, sucking her fingertip.

Isabel looked unconcerned. "Whatever."

"Come *on*. You don't carry a weapon like that unless you're intending to hunt bear, or something." Isabel didn't answer. Kelly looked at her. "Or unless you're afraid of someone."

"I'm not afraid," Isabel said, almost too calmly.

Kelly looked over her shoulder. Paula had finished making her bed and was on her way out of the room, and Angel seemed preoccupied with her own belongings. "You'd better put that away before someone else sees it," she whispered. "If Porter knew you'd brought a knife, he'd take it away from you."

"That would be too bad," Isabel said with a sigh. "It's great for cleaning fish and doing all sorts of camping chores." She fingered the leather hilt, decorated with hundreds of tiny, bright beads in an intricate pattern.

Kelly inched closer. "Where did you get a thing like that?"

"My grandfather. He made this ring for me too."

51

Isabel held up her right hand. The sunburst with the velvet-smooth turquoise stone.

"It's beautiful," Kelly said admiringly, then was suddenly struck by a realization. "Oh! You're American Indian of some sort!"

"Part Navaho." Isabel's rich brown eyes twinkled.

Kelly observed the knife. "May I see it?"

Deftly, Isabel flipped the flat of the blade in her palm so that the colorful grip faced Kelly. She accepted it carefully.

The knife was surprisingly heavy, solid in her hand. She didn't need to test its edge to know that it was razor-sharp. Her finger still throbbed softly—and she'd barely touched the blade.

As if reading her mind Isabel said, "It keeps a good edge." She took the knife back, with loving care wrapped it in a sweater, and placed it back inside the suitcase. "Well, I guess I'm ready. Are you done?"

Kelly nodded. "For now."

"Angel?" Isabel asked.

Kelly turned to jelly inside. She didn't normally snub people, but Angel was a tempting candidate for social exile.

Luckily, Angel didn't respond to Isabel's offer to join them. The girl seemed, in fact, totally absorbed in her own world, sitting cross-legged on her bed. Around the black cloud of her dress sat an array of bizarre objects—black crystals cupped in torn squares of tissue paper, a necklace with a large charm dangling at its middle, a book covered in black velvet and a half dozen other indiscernible items.

52

Isabel stepped closer. "What are those for?" She pointed at the crystals.

Angel continued moving objects around on her bed, as if seeking the perfect position for each. Without commenting, she picked up the necklace and draped it around her neck. On closer observation, Kelly could see that the charm was a miniature human head. More precisely, a skull fashioned from some sort of dull gray metal.

Angel lifted it in front of her face. "Now we are ready to begin," she told the skull in a deep voice.

And I have to sleep in the same room with this! Kelly cringed inside. "Come on," she said, tugging at Isabel's arm, suddenly anxious for the security of the rest of the group.

Isabel resisted. "Angel, do you want to come with us?"

"I have duties to perform," Angel intoned to the charm. "I must obey."

"Oh, brother," Kelly breathed, backing toward the door, visions of demon worship and blood-swilling cults swimming in her head.

But Isabel stood firm. She looked over the collection of trinkets, then slowly reached down toward the velvet book.

"I wouldn't touch anything if I were you," Kelly hissed in her ear. "You don't know where it's been." *Or what kind of curse it has on it.*

At the last possible moment, Angel noticed the motion of Isabel's hand. In a flash, she whisked the book out of reach, her dark eyes peering up at Isabel like glowing coals. *"Do not touch!"* Angel screeched.

Isabel blinked, looking surprised. "I was only curious to see what it was."

"My letters."

"You mean you keep a diary? Oh, well, I understand. That *is* private," Isabel murmured, giving the other girl a sympathetic smile. "I saw you writing on the bus. Do you record everything you see?"

Angel's sullen gaze dropped away. "I see all. Know all."

"Undoubtedly," Kelly said dryly. "Come on, Isabel. Please don't encourage her."

"I'm just interested."

"I don't think she wants to talk anymore. *Come on!*" Kelly urged.

Isabel glanced over her shoulder one last time at Angel, who was whispering with great urgency to her skull charm. Then Kelly tugged her out through the door.

The boys were taking far less care with their unpacking. Chris, in fact, had done nothing more than kick his gym bag beneath the bed and sprawl on top of the unmade mildew-stained mattress. He'd positioned the most crucial items in his bag where he could find them most easily. Now he had to wait for the others to leave the room before he could get at them.

If he pretended he was falling asleep again, these wimps wouldn't hassle him. Only little Kelly had been brave enough to dare waking him on the bus. They'd all witnessed his reaction then—and she was a girl.

From beneath lazily drooping lids, Chris waited, watching them.

Jeff—he was all right. Chris could understand him better than the others because of their common interest in sports. But Jeff didn't care the way he did. Cross country, wrestling were just assets to Jeff—a couple of sports to list on college application forms, to round out his super-achiever image. For Chris, football was his life. It was his meal ticket, the roof over his head, his future. Without it, he was nothing.

In his freshman year when Coach first approached him, telling him he was so talented Coach would be moving him straight up to varsity, Chris had planned everything. It was simple: he'd play his guts out for four years, then wait for the recruiters to flock around.

How many times had he seen it on TV? Some jock who could hardly put a sentence together, announcing at a press conference he'd at last chosen his college. *Chosen!* Like he had more juicy offers than he knew what to do with! Of course they'd *all* offer Chris "the Madman" Baxter a full four-year scholarship, but he'd hold out for UCLA. UCLA was his dream.

Well, he'd done everything he could to be the kind of player who'd appeal to college scouts, to the pros too. He'd made himself strong and bulked up, training with free weights and Nautilus machines until he'd become pretty damn awesome. Of course, he had a long way to go before he looked like those dudes in the muscle 'zines, with the ripped, greased look, but he was getting there. The trouble was, his grades, which had always been moderately good, were dropping. And he just couldn't seem to get a hold on his emotions these days. Every game, there were at least two monster fights, and he always seemed to be in the middle, taking a chunk out of someone—the other team, his own, it didn't matter anymore. His rage, once set off, was beyond his control. They all seemed to be against him—the coaches, his teammates, his parents, kids in the stands.

He'd begun to hate them. And his hate fed his need to succeed because only by succeeding could he show them he didn't need their friendship. But even though he'd been mentioned in *Sports Illustrated* as "a young athlete to watch" and the smaller schools were still interested, the more prestigious universities shied away from him. "Lacks discipline . . . off-balance," they said. "We don't need another street brawler."

However, Porter had come to him out of the blue with an offer of help. "Join my SAT crash course over vacation. If you score even moderately high on the test, it will show the recruiters a different kind of discipline," the teacher said. "Everyone will realize there's more to you than uncontrolled muscle." It seemed strange to him that the only one who still gave a damn what happened to him was a history teacher he'd gotten a C from a year earlier. But by this time Chris was getting desperate. And when Porter had offered to let him take the course for half the usual tuition, he'd signed up.

Chris lifted one eyelid to cautiously observe the others in the room, staying well clear of his bed—Jeff, Nathan, Brian. Well, Jeff was all right. If he hadn't been rich, he might have been the kind of guy he'd like for a friend—if that mattered, and it didn't.

Brian was rich too. He'd heard his father had bought him a ticket to the Air Force Academy. He'd always considered Brian a wimp anyway, but that sewed things up. If you couldn't earn your own spot—you didn't deserve it.

Nathan, though, was a waste from day one. Nathan ate crap for lunch—bologna-and-ketchup sandwiches on white bread, potato chips, tons of the greasy things, all topped off with a chocolate bar—pure metabolic poison. *You are what you eat,* Chris always believed.

But other than the fact Nathan was a walking refuse heap, Chris couldn't figure out what made him tick or why he chose the friends he did. Drifting, older types who dropped out of school as soon as they hit sixteen.

Still appearing to doze, Chris watched Nathan sort through his stuff. *Man, this dude's thought of everything!* mused Chris.

Heavy-metal tapes for the little recorder Porter had asked everyone to bring, even though prerecorded tapes were taboo, a couple dozen Hershey bars—also on the Do Not Bring list—several decks of playing cards, at least one six-pack of beer, assorted miniature liquor bottles, a couple dozen condoms . . .

Condoms? Chris almost laughed out loud. The guy *might* have room in there for one change of clothes, which meant he'd be wearing the same filthy jeans and shirt for at least three days—and he thought some chick was going to let him within a foot of her? Fat chance, fool.

Girls.

They'd been one of the big reasons he'd gone out for football in middle school, had started working out, shaping his body to rid himself of even the last traces of adolescent baby fat. Sadly, like the athletic scouts, the girls had backed off too, after an initial, delicious flurry of interest.

Afraid. They were all afraid of him.

Waiting to be left alone in the room, Chris closed his eyes all the way, shutting out the pain, the loneliness.

Chapter 4

By noon, a crackling fire had been built in the fire-place and everyone—or almost everyone—was assembled around the long picnic-style table in the lounge.

Lunch was sandwiches made with deli ham, turkey, roast beef, two kinds of cheese, onions, sliced tomatoes, lettuce, and gobs of mayo on grinder rolls. Since Jeff and Nathan had made them, they were humongous, and one was proving to be more than enough for Kelly.

She ate quickly, as hungry as the rest of the group from the long drive. Except for Angel. She sat with the group but refused to touch any food. Rocking gently on the bench, she lapsed into a low, monotonous, unintelligible chant. Once in a while, she would crack open her diary to scribble a few words.

Kelly tried to ignore her by concentrating on eating and her new surroundings.

Apparently Porter had stocked up on a generous supply of food in advance, including a 25-pound turkey for their Thanksgiving dinner the next day. A refrigerator located at one end of the room ran off its own generator.

If there's enough power for a fridge, why not for lights? Kelly wondered, frowning at the kerosene lanterns lined up near the door. She could practically taste their rancid oily smell from here and wasn't looking forward to darkness. The cabin's isolation was even more complete than she'd expected from the drive.

The outside door swung open, and everyone looked up from the table. Chris walked in. With Porter's permission, he'd been working out in the clearing, hefting boulders instead of his usual weights. His dark skin still streaming with sweat, he took a seat on the wooden bench beside Kelly.

"Looks good!" he boomed, helping himself to a sandwich with each hand.

"They are." Wishing he'd washed off in the lake before joining them, Kelly gave him a dim smile. He smelled like a mobile locker room.

Porter surveyed the young faces around the table from his position at its head, then wiped his mouth with a paper napkin. "You have thirty minutes to finish eating and wash your dishes, then we'll start right to work. Shall we say—everyone assembles at one-thirty, right here." He rose from his seat, quickly rinsed his plate and coffee cup, and left the cabin without further explanation.

Nathan shot to his feet as soon as the door closed at Porter's back. "Dessert time!" he crowed, chuckling as he disappeared into the boys' room. A couple of minutes later he was back with a Hershey bar.

"Contraband," Jeff observed. "What else have you got stashed in there?"

"Anything your little heart desires," boasted Nathan with glee. "For a price."

"Oh, give me a break," Kelly moaned.

Chris eyed Nathan critically. "What were you doing in that room?"

"Doing?" Nathan mumbled innocently around a bite of candy.

Chris's wide face darkened. "You damn well stay out of my stuff!"

"Man," Nathan muttered, "I wouldn't *touch* your stuff."

"If I find anything missing—"

"Just cool it, okay? I'm not that stupid."

Both boys fell silent, but a steamy tension hung in the room where a few minutes earlier the air had been damp and cold from being so long unheated. Kelly looked nervously from Chris to Nathan. Should she say something to cool things down? Should she try to find Porter before the two boys flew at each other's throat?

Angel stopped chanting to whisper something to her charm. Isabel stared down at her plate, uncharacteristically silent.

Glancing across the table at Jeff, Kelly willed him to play the peacemaker. But he seemed to be giving his food a great deal of attention.

A nervous knot gripped her stomach. *He's avoiding me. He doesn't like me, and he knows I'm watching him, and he's trying to tell me in a subtle way to get lost! I'm going to die.*

In fact, the only people in the room who seemed to be oblivious to the potential explosion were Brian and Paula. At the far end of the table, their heads were lowered in private conversation. Brian shook his

61

head at Paula, as if disagreeing with something she'd said, then shook his head a second time, more emphatically.

Picking at her bread crumbs, Kelly wished Porter would come back. Didn't he realize he'd assembled a powder keg of personalities at Deep Creek? *He* was the goddamn teacher around here! Wasn't it his responsibility to keep everyone in line?

Angel began chanting again beneath her breath.

"Quit that!" Brian snapped, rubbing his forehead. "You're driving me nuts. I can't think with that noise!"

Angel stopped. She gazed at him and broke into a ghoulish smile.

Kelly found herself preferring a morbid Angel to this new black-lipped smirking creature, but she hated to see anyone totally friendless. "She's not really bothering anyone," she murmured, trying to smooth things over.

"Brian's right," Jeff argued. "She's giving me the creeps." He looked at Angel. "What are you trying to prove with all this mumbo jumbo—that you're some kind of witch or something?"

"Or something," answered Angel, deadpan. Her thickly mascaraed eyes swerved toward Brian. "I know you."

Everyone turned to look at him, and for a moment the room was completely silent.

"What are you talking about?" Brian demanded, scowling at her.

"I know you," she repeated.

Paula leaned forward, her lips twisted up in an uncertain smile. "What do you mean, you *know* him? You don't even go to Thomaston."

Angel trailed a considering look over the blonde cheerleader. "You—are—a—beast," she proclaimed solemnly.

The color drained from Paula's cheeks. *"What* did you call me?"

"She called you a beast," Nathan said helpfully, removing his sunglasses to polish them. "Mind if I excuse myself, children? I hate family squabbles, got enough of them at home." He left the table, quickly slipping back into the boys' room and shutting the door after him.

Chris stared at the closed door as he reached for his third sandwich.

"Brian," Paula whined, "tell her she can't call me names."

But he just looked blankly at Paula.

"Where do you know Brian from?" Kelly asked, curious.

Angel gazed down at her skull, as if speaking to it rather than to anyone at the table. "I know you . . . from another life."

Paula shot up from the table, eyes ablaze, mouth gaping open. Before she could say anything, Brian reached out, clamping a restraining hand on her arm.

"It doesn't matter," he said in a distinct voice, fixing Paula with a meaningful stare. "Understand? I'll do it."

She tightened her lips over unuttered words and granted him a thin smile of satisfaction. Kelly would have given anything to know what sort of points Paula had secretly won during the exchange, and why—but Isabel nudged her in the ribs just them. She looked up to see Chris leaving the table, heading into the boys' room.

Drawing an anxious breath, Kelly listened, her nerves prickling with apprehension. Nathan and Chris were alone in there! No sound came from inside the room. "Bri, maybe you and Jeff ought to—you know." Kelly gestured toward the door.

A loud crash brought the kids to their feet. Kelly and Isabel, being on the open side of the table, were the first on the scene.

Chris had pinned Nathan to the wall by his throat. Nathan's eyes bulged like those of a dead fish, his sneakers scuffling frantically against the air, a foot off the ground. The football player's face was contorted with fury, his menacing eyes boring into Nathan, powerful fists knotted beneath the other boy's chin.

"Stop it!" Kelly shrieked. "God, you're killing him!"

The situation was dire enough to prompt Jeff and Brian to action, despite their fear for their own personal safety. Jeff leaped on Chris's back, angling his forearm across his muscled throat from behind. Brian dragged down on the thick wrists, using his full body weight, but with little effect.

"Stop it, Chris!" Kelly shouted in his ear.

Isabel screamed in his other, "Let him go! Let him go!"

At last, they seemed to get his attention—if not loosen his crushing grip on Nathan. Chris's crazed glare turned on Kelly, and she found she couldn't speak, her mouth was so dry with fright. She'd never seen anyone go berserk like this, and it terrified her—the uncontrollable force of this boy she'd gone to school with all these years. What had set him off?

Then somehow Isabel wedged herself between Kelly and the tangle of four boys and began talking in a soft, soothing tone, her eyes pleading. "Christopher, don't hurt him. He won't say anything, now that he knows. He was just curious."

Knows what? Kelly thought wildly.

But as if by magic, the sweet sound of Isabel's voice loosened the thick black fingers mangling Nathan's shirtfront. His scrawny body slid down the wall between Chris's hands.

Choking and coughing raggedly, gasping for air, Nathan staggered out of range. "Man," he croaked, "man, what's *with* you?"

"Stay out o' my stuff," Chris rumbled deep from within his heaving chest, his eyes afire, fists kneading at his side as if still holding a piece of Nathan.

"Yeah, sure. You got it." Nathan staggered out of the room.

Grabbing his gym bag from on top of his bed, Chris crammed a mess of disheveled clothing inside, tossed the bag beneath the bed frame, and threw himself down on the mattress with his back to the others.

Feeling a little dizzy, Kelly let out a long breath she hadn't realized she'd been holding. "Oh, God," she whispered hoarsely, "I thought he was going to *kill* him. I really did."

Looking away, Isabel muttered something that

sounded like: "It's not *him* you should be concerned with."

"What?" Kelly asked.

Suddenly, there were steps outside the bedroom and Porter poked his head through the doorway. "This table is filthy. All of you come help Nathan clean up. He's apparently the only one around here who knows how to follow directions."

And so Kelly didn't have a chance to ask Isabel again what she'd meant. If she had, they all might have survived Thanksgiving vacation.

Nathan was still shaky from the fight. A bruise had formed over his collarbone where Chris Baxter's iron-hard fists had dug painfully into his flesh. Well, never mind. The good news was, at least now he had something on Chris. He just had to figure out how to use the information to his best advantage.

I'll pay you back! he thought with satisfaction.

At last, everyone finished putting away dishes and wrapping leftover sandwiches. The group reassembled around the long wooden table, Porter standing at one end. "You're here for one reason," he announced, instantly quieting their chatter with an icy look. *"To work.* I can help you work . . . and learn, but I won't be there to take the SAT for you."

"No kidding," someone murmured.

Nathan snickered, amused.

Porter peered down the double row of innocent faces, his stony expression concealing whether he'd also heard. "I'll just say this, if you're not willing to work with me, you have one alternative. It's called

66

unskilled labor. That's all you have to choose from if you don't go to college these days. On the other hand, some of you have more at stake than just being admitted to the community college—you know who you are. There's a certain score you need on this test."

Porter looked over his glasses at Jeff. "It takes a combined verbal-math score of fourteen hundred to get into Harvard. If the applicant has a 'legacy'—family members who attended before him—maybe twelve hundred will do. No less." Jeff squirmed on his bench, studied the knuckles of one hand. Porter's unyielding gaze shifted to Chris. "UCLA looks for a nice round thousand, even from its would-be athletic stars. The rest of the schools"—he waved his hand dismissively—"they're in-between somewhere. Except for Thomaston Community College. T.C.C. will be tickled pink with a seven hundred—total." On cue, he raised a brow at Nathan.

A low laugh circled the table.

Nathan grinned, shrugged. He didn't give a damn about prestige. At least he'd be in school, have a roof over his head. Even Thomaston had some dorms.

"We'll start with the verbal sections," Porter continued briskly. "Every SAT has two of these, thirty minutes each. Twenty-five antonyms, twenty analogies, fifteen sentence completions and twenty-five reading comprehensions. Don't get too uptight thinking about the first part of the test—it's nothing but a vocabulary quiz in disguise. If you can remember your social security number, you can pull a four-fifty. If you can recall ten of your friends' telephone numbers, you can get an easy six hundred. And if you memorized the periodic table in chemistry, chances are you have the potential for acing verbal with a perfect eight hundred.''

Nathan beamed. Hey, things were looking up. He had avoided taking chemistry because he'd heard it was hard and boring, so he'd opted for yet another industrial arts. He didn't have ten friends, or even acquaintances, who'd willingly give him their phone numbers. However, if atmospheric conditions were just right, he could rattle off his social security number with the best of them!

Porter was passing out photocopied booklets. ''Let's begin with a sample question from the antonym section.''

Nathan scanned the first sheet. At the top, it said:

WANTON:
   (A) incestuous
   (B) big
   (C) detain
   (D) absolutely empty
   (E) moral

Nathan groaned, shoving the papers away. ''I never heard of this friggin' word, how the hell am I supposed to figure out what it means?''

Porter looked at him. ''By the time our five days are up, you'll know it and many more twice as complex, Mr. Grant.''

''You expect us to *memorize* the friggin' dictionary or something?''

''I expect you to open your *friggin'* mind and let

in some fresh air,'' Porter remarked dryly. ''A few specks of knowledge might drift in with it.''

Nathan shook his head. What a load of BS.

Then Jeff reached over and laid a gentle hand on his back. ''Remember your old man.'' he whispered.

That was all Nathan needed to hear. Yeah, the alternative to college was scary. He could see himself in twenty years—hell, maybe only ten—a duplicate of his father. A fat slob, full-blown alkie, no friends, except ones he'd rather lose, like Seth and Muncie— the dangerous kind that showed up when you least expected, made trouble you got blamed for. He *had* to give this a shot.

''Okay,'' Nathan demanded, ''so like how do I cram thousands of words I never heard of into my head?''

''You don't,'' Porter said, a sly smile in his eyes. ''For a question such as this one, you'll use logic— which might be a stretch for some of you, but it's your best bet. First of all, we eliminate C because it's a different part of speech from the other answers—a verb rather than an adjective. Next, we cross out D, *absolutely empty,* because it's a stupid answer. If something is empty, there's nothing there—pure and simple. It can't be *more* empty. That leaves A, B, and E.''

Kelly raised her hand. ''You haven't said anything about the meaning of the word at all,'' she complained. ''Some of us may have heard it used before.''

''True,'' Porter agreed. ''But because there will be unfamiliar words that even a brilliant scholar such as you, Miss Peterson, will find unfamiliar, we'll continue to examine this technique."

"Technique?" Jeff interrupted. "All you're doing is teaching us how to cheat the system."

"No, he isn't," Brian said thoughtfully. "He's showing us how to narrow down the possibilities by using our heads. He's not giving us answers or anything."

Jeff looked unsure. "I guess."

"I believe Mr. Lopez understands my method." Porter's tiny eyes looked pleased and strangely bright behind the thick lenses as he stared at Brian. Almost feverish, Nathan thought. And he was glad he was no longer the object of the teacher's attention.

Brian nodded stiffly. "Maybe I do."

"Ah, yes. I thoroughly enjoy mind games—the more challenging the better. Before these five days are through, you'll realize just how seriously I take my games. *Now*"—Porter nearly shouted the word, looking for a moment like a mad scientist—"back to the matter at hand. Let's consider the SATs a game. We'll say that this particular question is located in the last third of the exam. What about B—*big?*"

Isabel hesitantly raised her hand. "Since each section starts with easy questions and ends up with hard ones, you're saying that *wanton* is in the most difficult part of the test."

"Exactly."

"Then *wanton* wouldn't mean big, because that's too easy an answer."

"Very good, Miss Smith."

Nathan couldn't believe it. The schmuck had nar-

rowed the odds down to just two possible answers—
and he still didn't know what the stupid word meant!
Rad!

"I know what incestuous means," Nathan volunteered.

"You do?" Porter raised both brows this time.

Nathan grinned, pleased with himself. "Yeah.
Messing with your little sister is incestuous and that's
*im*moral—not to mention sick."

"Precisely. So the two remaining answers—incestuous and moral—are related. They are antonyms—
opposites. But moral has a much wider meaning, so
it will likely be the answer because there are more
opportunities for antonyms. As it turns out—*moral* is
an antonym for *wanton* and is therefore the correct
answer."

Kelly shot an amazed look at Jeff, who still didn't
appear convinced of Porter's system. Well, *she* saw
nothing wrong with psyching out the Educational
Testing Service. Porter hadn't broken one rule or suggested by anything that he'd said that they should
cheat.

"Next," Porter continued, "the tape recorders."
Everyone had brought theirs to the table as requested.
He asked them to turn to the middle portion of their
brochures. "This is your word list, with definitions."

Chris let out a low whistle.

"Oh, man," groaned Nathan.

"It's not as bad as it looks," Porter said quickly.
"There are only about six hundred words. Some of
them you already know."

"Six hundred," Angel whispered to her charm. "Six thousand, six million . . . billion . . . trillion."

Kelly rolled her eyes. *I hope your breath melts the goddamn thing,* she thought, imagining she could see evil vapors wafting from those black-glossed lips.

"For each of the words on this list," Porter went on, "we will create a titillating sentence, something that you'll have trouble forgetting because the image it creates is so strong. Take our first example—wanton. Who can suggest a sentence?"

Brian coughed, then said solemnly, "They made wanton love in the meadow."

"That certainly sticks in *my* mind." Nathan cried, directing a leer at Isabel.

She hastily averted her eyes.

Kelly felt sorry for the quiet Indian girl. Having received no encouragement from Kelly earlier in the day, Nathan was now testing the romantic waters with someone new.

"That's good," Porter shocked everyone by saying. "But we could make our sentence even more memorable. Remember, the more personalized the sentence, the more likely you'll be able to recall it when you need it. How about this one—*Jeffrey made wanton love to the beautiful green-eyed cat-goddess . . . in a tub of won-ton soup.*"

"That's wanton all right!" Nathan shrieked appreciatively, pounding the table.

Chris grinned shyly at Kelly over his shoulder, as if he suspected she must be embarrassed—since she was the only green-eyed girl present and the cat-goddess bit had been an obvious reference to her role in *Cats*. Jeff was desperately trying to avoid her glance, his face flushed. But Kelly didn't really mind. The joke was almost an ideal setup, placing her in a flattering spotlight—goddess!—bringing up the question of romance with Jeff. And that sounded very nice indeed.

For the next hour, each SAT group member retreated to a separate corner of the room to work on part of the list of definitions. They created humorous, sometimes bawdy sample sentences that frequently featured people they knew. Porter passed out blank audio tapes and asked them to record each word, definition, and sample sentence.

For "pensive," Jeff worked out a cute pun on the thoughtful state of Pensive-ania. Nathan used "magnanimous" in a sentence with a *magnificent*—his word—part of his anatomy, describing how generously he'd share it with any interested female, only to have Jeff claim that Nathan could be sued for false advertising. Paula created a sentence for "captious": *His captious attitude forced her to take him captive to prove she was right.* Of course that prompted Nathan to offer himself in bondage, then Angel started getting a dangerous gleam in her eye, and Porter hastily called an end to their first work session.

"All right," Porter said, summoning everyone back to the table. "We'll be dividing up the remaining words tomorrow. By noon, the group will have completed recording all the SAT vocabulary. Every time you have a free moment, listen to a tape. Sing or rap the words if it helps. Visualize the sentences. Swap tapes until you've heard all of them several times." He looked even more disapproving than his normal self. "From what I've heard today, it shouldn't be difficult."

They all laughed. Some of the samples had admittedly gotten pretty raunchy, or else downright sick. But Kelly had to admit that Porter was right, the words definitely stuck in her mind. Maybe he knew what he was doing after all.

Chapter 5

By five o'clock, it was beginning to get dark. The woods seemed to close in around the cabin at Deep Creek Lake, making it feel even smaller than it had in the daylight, defenseless against whatever might be lurking out there. A chilly damp mist drifted up from the lake, settling in Jeff's bones. He felt cold from the inside out, and restless, unwilling to remain in the cabin although it offered at least a meager stuffy, wood-smoke heat from the fireplace. A disturbing tension lingered in the lounge. He supposed it was due to Chris and Nathan's fight. They were still projecting deadly glares at each other across the room.

Most of all, though, Jeff didn't think he could take being shut up inside any longer in the cabin with Kelly without telling her how nuts he was about her. The way she walked, moved her hands so delicately, like a dancer, when she spoke, the way she tilted her head, making her green eyes sparkle in the firelight—she was driving him bonkers! He had to get out.

"Can we build a campfire?" he asked Porter, remembering the ashes in the clearing. It would give him something to do, an excuse for going outside.

"Go ahead. Just keep the sparks away from the building."

Porter had commandeered Nathan and Paula as kitchen slaves, to prepare the evening meal. The others had an hour to themselves before supper would be ready.

Starting for the door, Jeff heard Brian ask, "I saw what looks like a boat house, down by the edge of the lake . . . are we allowed to use the boats?"

"There's only one, a wooden rowboat. But I guess you can take it out," Porter mumbled absentmindedly, not bothering to look up from his notes. "Wear a life jacket. Stay near the shore."

Brian nodded and picked up his jacket from the peg near the door.

Standing in front of the open refrigerator, Paula solemnly watched him leave, as if wishing Porter had chosen someone else for kitchen duty so she'd be free to go along.

Jeff followed Brian outside, stopping to observe the other boy as he disappeared down the shadowy path toward the lake. He liked Brian all right. They weren't really friends, but he respected him. Brian Lopez was the solid, capable sort of guy who'd probably become "Top Gun" in flight school, rack up medals if ever in combat. Later in life, he could see him becoming a district attorney, U.S. congressman . . . judge . . . whatever. He was straight as they came and a hard worker. Jeff's dad would love him.

Suddenly, Jeff became aware that he wasn't alone. He turned.

Kelly and Isabel had just stepped outside. As soon as Kelly realized Jeff was looking at her, she glanced away—but not before melting his heart with her gorgeous emerald eyes.

Cat-goddess. He shivered, dragged down a deep breath for courage. Man, playing it cool around Kelly was going to be even harder than he'd expected.

During the afternoon session, they'd sat directly across from each other, same seats as during lunch. On several occasions Kelly's knee had brushed his, driving him up the wall. He wanted her so bad it physically hurt. But what could he do? If he touched her—*really* touched her the way he yearned to—he knew he'd think of nothing but her for the next four days. This crash course, his last hope, would be a waste.

To make himself look busy, he started gathering tinder from the shrubs closest to the cabin, working his way gradually into the woods. When Jeff returned to the clearing, his arms full of twigs, bark, and assorted branches, Kelly and Isabel were seated in a pair of rustic log-and-rope chairs. Brian and Chris stood over them, talking. Jeff went about his work, wondering why Brian had changed his mind about taking out the rowboat.

Silently, he arranged the wood in a precise pile, concentrating on what he was doing to help block out the way Kelly's musical voice danced among the trees then leapt back at him, like a mischievous wood nymph's laughter.

"Hi," a voice said a moment later.

It's Kelly, standing right next to me, he thought. *I'm dead meat.*

"Oh, hi," he answered smoothly.

"Need these? Or do you get your fires started the old-fashioned way?"

As he took the wooden kitchen matches from her, he couldn't help smiling just a little. She probably didn't realize how flirtatious she sounded. "I wouldn't know what to do with a flint, if that's what you mean," he murmured, observing his feet.

"You were never a Boy Scout?"

He was sweating inside his flannel shirt, even though it was close to freezing outside. "No, never."

"Gee, and you seem to handle yourself so well in the woods," Kelly remarked off-handedly, flipping a mass of red curls over her shoulder.

He choked, coughed, forced himself not to look at her by shifting his glance to a rock, then a tree stump. And all the time he was thinking—*Man, would I love to handle her in the woods!*

No, knock it off! Jeff chided himself. He was beginning to sound as horny as Nathan. Kelly deserved better. She was no ordinary girl.

"Guess just about anyone can light a stupid match," he grumbled.

She frowned at him. "Is something wrong, Jeff?"

"Nope."

"I hope what Porter said in there—you know, the won-ton soup bit—didn't bother you."

"Hey, no sweat. That's *his* fantasy, not mine." Why had he said that? He didn't want to ruin his chances of *ever* getting together with her. What if Kelly thought she turned him off? "I mean, you know, maybe my choice of soup would be tomato

. . . or chicken noodle.'' Jeff allowed her a brief, not too encouraging smile.

She giggled, looking relieved.

During their conversation, he'd struck a dozen or more matches, most of which blew out before he could touch them to the tinder. At last one held its flame, and a few sticks began to glow red. A deep blood red, he thought for some reason. Crimson sparks floated up into the black sky.

The lake was now invisible between the tree trunks. The circle of darkness grew solid around the clearing, almost like a wall cutting them off from the rest of the world.

Isabel, Brian, and Chris edged closer to the fire. Jeff was pretty sure that, like him, none of them felt completely at ease here. Tonight—although none of them knew very much about the others—they'd sleep together under one roof, with only mud-cemented logs and each other for protection. Already the winter birds were settling down for the night, and the sounds of nocturnal animals snuffling in the underbrush seemed to be growing closer. Or was it his imagination?

Jeff squatted beside the fire, held his palms out toward the flames to warm them. Hesitantly, Kelly sat down beside him, her shadow Isabel crouching next to her. Brian seemed at a loss without Paula around, glancing at the cabin, out in the direction of the lake, back again at the fire. At last he also took a seat on the ground. Chris alone remained standing above the fire. He seemed transfixed by the flames—the popping wood and sweet smoke rising in clouds—unaware of the rest of them. Jeff wondered, not for the first time, if he was on drugs.

Jeff remembered Isabel's words as she'd tried to calm Chris: *He won't say anything . . . now that he knows."*

Then out of the shadows, Angel materialized. She was wearing a long, black robe, a knotted black silk scarf tied around her pale forehead and frenzied hair.

No one said a word, and for a long moment it was as if they were all suspended in time. Waiting. Waiting for something terrible to happen.

Finally, Kelly drew an audible breath. "Creepy, isn't it?"

Jeff laughed, as if he hadn't been thinking the same thing. "It's not bad."

"Know any ghost stories?"

Angel's eyes glowed dimly across the licking red fire-tongues.

I'll bet she knows plenty, Kelly thought.

"Naw," Jeff said, sitting back on his butt. "I don't go for that sort of stuff. It's silly, really. Getting all worked up about things that go bump in the night."

Kelly loved a good scary tale, though. She'd read every one of Stephen King's novels. She liked *It* best, and *Cycle of the Werewolf* had kept her sleepless for two whole nights last summer. Was that where *her* dream wolf had come from?

"What about you, Isabel?" she asked.

The honey-skinned girl hesitated, then nodded. "I know a lot of stories my grandfather told me."

"She's part Indian," Kelly explained to the others.

"Really?" Brian asked, interested.

"Navaho, mostly," Isabel replied. "But I have an Irish grandmother."

Kelly was glad Nathan wasn't here. He'd have made a crass joke about redskins and Irish whiskey not mixing.

"Tell us an Indian ghost story," Kelly begged.

Isabel looked around the circle. Her glance stopped on Brian, and their eyes locked. "I'll tell you one about Deep Creek Lake."

Brian blinked, as if surprised, then looked away from her. "You must know lots of Indian stories, stuff about your own tribe," he mumbled.

"I like this one better," she insisted, smoothing the long, straight strands of luxurious hair away from her cheek. "It's a slightly different one than most people read in their history texts." She crossed her ankles, gracefully folding her legs beneath her. Closing her eyes, she recited in a hushed voice that barely rose above the whoosh of the night wind in the tree tops:

"A very long time ago, or not so long at all, there was a tribe called the Susquehana. They were a peaceful people who lived in these hills, planting seed in the spring, then moving their families to the Chesapeake Bay to fish during the warmest months while the crops grew wild. And each fall they'd return here to harvest and make ready for winter.

"For many, many years they lived happily in this way, until a controversy arose between them and a group of white settlers near the bay where the tribe summered. The whites believed that a Susquehana had killed a white town member. Probably no one will ever know if the accusation was true. But the white men were so outraged, they armed themselves, formed a vigilante group, and mounted a surprise attack on the Susquehana village under cover of darkness.''

Isabel's voice grew even softer. ''Virtually the entire tribe—every child, every woman and man—was annihilated that night in the bloody massacre. Only two remained, a young Indian maiden and her lover who had been off by themselves.''

Kelly felt a lump grow in her throat. ''How horrible,'' she murmured. She wished Jeff would put his arm around her, to ward off the chill that had nothing to do with the wind off the lake. ''What happened to them?''

Isabel opened her eyes slowly, her lovely face reflecting infinite sadness in the flickering red firelight. ''They loved each other deeply, but were filled with sorrow at the loss of their families and friends. Together, they returned to their tribe's lake in the hills.''

Isabel's voice rose dramatically. ''Now, the Susquehana believed that on the underside of the lake was another world—that of the spirit-god Gweemush. Gweemush ruled over the dead and, while you lived, over your soul. It was said that if you looked into the water on a moonless night you would see the reflection of your soul. Many were tempted to try, for learning the truth of all you are or might ever be—your future—could be very valuable. But it could also prove dangerous. The powerful Gweemush was greedy, and he had been known to steal the soul of the living if given the opportunity.''

Kelly could barely stand the suspense. Her nerve ends were prickling like crazy. ''What *happened* to them?'' she cried. ''Hurry up!''

Isabel shook her head forlornly. ''The lovers looked into the lake and saw . . . nothing—''

''Nothing?''

''Which meant only one thing to them. Gweemush had captured their souls and, as much as they loved life and wanted to be together, they must join their tribe in death. Holding hands, they obeyed the evil god and walked into Deep Creek Lake until the water lapped over their heads. Legend claims you can still see their agonized souls, floating in the mists over the lake on a night just like this—calling out to each other, lamenting their fate.''

Isabel gazed up into the dark branches overhead, her eyes moist with emotion, and no one spoke for a long time.

Kelly thought, *Either this girl is a better actress than I am, or she's a teensy bit wacko.*

Kelly looked across the fire at Brian, expecting to see him grinning at her, thinking the same thing. But his face was drawn and white.

''Oh, Bri,'' she teased, ''lighten up. I can't believe you fell for a silly old ghost story''

''Knock it off!'' he grumbled, stood up, and plodded off toward the cabin.

Surprised by his reaction, Kelly turned to Jeff. ''It wasn't *that* scary, was it?''

He cleared his throat, looking embarrassed, and changed the subject. "Care to go for a swim?"

He can't be serious, she thought. "Sure," she answered, laughing. "Why not?"

For a second, Jeff looked hesitant. Then he impulsively jumped up and, grinning, grabbed her by the wrists and started dragging her toward the lake.

"I was kidding, I was kidding!" Kelly shrieked, her heart racing, head whirling with confused, warm feelings, digging in her heels to hinder his progress.

With very little effort, Jeff threw her over his shoulder and stalked off between the dark tree trunks.

"Help!" Kelly shouted to those left behind in the clearing. "For God's sake stop this lunatic!"

After Jeff had carried off Kelly, Chris looked thoughtfully down at Isabel, then, without a word, followed Brian into the cabin. Only Isabel and Angel remained seated by the fire.

The Indian girl gazed into the flames, and a tear trailed down her honeyed cheek, dropping from the point of her chin onto her folded hands. "I don't know what else to do," she whispered.

Angel nodded.

Chapter 6

The chill air blew straight through her turtleneck and heavy sweater, but she was so depressed she didn't want to be around the others after supper—especially Jeff. Nathan, unfortunately, hadn't gotten the message and followed her outside.

"Where'd old Porter go?" he asked, picking ground beef from between his teeth with a twig.

Kelly dejectedly jabbed a stick at the glowing logs on the campfire. "He's reading in his room."

To her everlasting disappointment, Jeff had come to his senses before they plunged into the lake. Carrying her over his muscular shoulder, he'd actually raced into the water's edge up to his ankles. Kelly shrieked, giggled, yelled for help, not really caring whether anyone stopped her kidnapper, delirious with joy simply because Jeff was finally paying attention to her.

But he *had* stopped—the jerk. He'd set her down on dry ground with gentlemanly care, mumbled something about needing to listen to his vocab tape, and left her standing there in a daze with a stupid grin on her lips.

She could have killed him!

Five minutes later she stopped imagining unique

forms of torture for him and started wondering what she'd done wrong. Or said. Or if her breath had grossed him out.

"The hell with him," she muttered.

"What's that, snuggle bunny?" Nathan asked with a smirk.

Kelly leaned back against her elbows and looked up at the starless sky, trying to blank out everything but its endless black emptiness. "Leave me alone."

"As you wish, my love." But Nathan didn't go away.

The cabin door opened. Out came Paula and Brian, their arms around each other's waists, then Isabel and Angel, Chris, and Jeff. Jeff, bless his little stone heart, was still listening to a tape through his earphones.

"We're going to roast marshmallows!" Isabel announced cheerily, waving a bag of Jet-Puffeds.

"I'm game," Nathan offered with less enthusiasm than he might have earlier in the day. By now only Angel hadn't spurned his lewd advances—but that was, as far as Kelly had noticed, because he hadn't made any to her.

"Toss the bag over here," Brian called. He elbowed Paula playfully in the ribs. "Might as well pork out."

She gave him a swift, silencing look. He shrugged.

Angel came over and silently held out her hand, long black fingernails curving up in a cup.

Observing her face closely as if still trying to place her, Brian took a few marshmallows out of the bag and gingerly laid them on her palm. Then he passed the bag to Chris, who grabbed a fistful before pulling off Jeff's earphones to get his attention and shoving the bag at him.

Soon they were all sitting in a circle, sticks poised over the fire.

Nathan liked to impale two marshmallows at a time on his stick, then thrust them straight into the flame to make them catch on fire. After observing his technique, Angel copied him, allowing hers to blaze gloriously, crinkle up, and sizzle until thoroughly charred.

Kelly tried not to watch the girl's gleeful expression, sure she was witnessing the birth of a pyromaniac.

"I need to go to the can," Angel muttered to no one in particular.

Kelly looked up, startled. It was the only coherent sentence she'd heard from her all day. With reluctance, she started to get up from the ground. "You can't go alone. Porter's rules."

"Paula," Angel intoned to her skull charm. "Paula will come with me."

Paula's jaw went slack. "Me? Why me?"

Instead of answering, Angel stood up and started walking away, into the woods.

Paula and Kelly exchanged looks. Kelly could see the cheerleader didn't want the honor any more than she did.

"Look, why don't you just go with her," Brian coaxed his girlfriend. "I'm sure she's harmless. She seems lonely. Maybe you can get her to talk to people instead of inanimate objects."

Paula grimaced. "I *loath* that creature," she hissed.

"For me?" Brian gave her a squeeze.

Her blue eyes melted into adoring pools. Obediently, she reached for one of the lanterns that sat beside the fire. "I'll be right back," she said. "Hey, Angel, wait up!"

Nathan watched them disappear amidst the trees. "That's one wild chick," he commented appreciatively.

Kelly laughed, knowing he couldn't mean Paula. She studied Brian for a moment. During his last exchange with Paula, she'd again felt as if they were speaking in some kind of secret language. It irritated her, the way it did when someone whispered behind her back and she was sure they were talking about her.

"What was that all about?" she demanded, her voice sounding sharper than she'd intended.

"Nothing," Brian muttered, jamming a plump marshmallow on his stick.

Kelly rolled her eyes. "It had to be *something*. You gave in to her, Bri, didn't you? This afternoon, at the table. Not the academy, I hope!"

"Naw, nothing like that." He reached over and ruffled her hair. "You worry too much. I'll take care of everything." But before he turned away what looked like a flash of fear glimmered from his soft eyes.

Kelly was aware that the others were watching them, listening intently but unwilling to interrupt. All but Jeff. He had returned to his vocab tape, his eyes shut in concentration.

Suddenly, Isabel slapped her gooey stick against the dirt. "Brian, don't do it!"

She hadn't been imagining things. Something *was* going on. "Don't do what?" Kelly squealed, exasperated. "Why is everyone talking in riddles?

"Shut up!" Brian shouted at Isabel.

"No!" Isabel's eyes were intense, her voice taut. "If you go ahead with—"

"I said shut the hell up!" Brian jumped to his feet. "You don't know what you're talking about. Nothing's going to happen!" His hands were shaking at his sides. He drew them into fists, fighting for control, staring in the direction Paula and Angel had disappeared into the trees. "Don't you think they should be back by now?"

Kelly sighed, utterly confused but feeling for him nevertheless. "You're doing the same thing to Paula she always does to you," she observed quietly. "Don't be so possessive."

He nodded, sitting down again. "Guess you're right. She's got to learn you can take togetherness too far."

But ten minutes later, the two girls still weren't back.

"I'm going to look for them," Brian announced, standing up abruptly.

"You can't go alone," Kelly pointed out. "Porter's rules."

"Which also means *you* can't go with me, lady."

"I can if another guy's with us." Without giving herself a chance to think about what she was doing, Kelly strode over to Jeff, lifted the spongy earphone

89

off of his right ear. "We need you, Mr. SAT. Come on."

He looked annoyed. "Why?"

"Paula and Angel aren't back yet. We're going to look for them. Hop to, dude!"

She hadn't meant to sound as if it were an order, but her impatience with Jeff had reached its limit. Why didn't he like her? She was a likable person. She had lots of friends, and she knew, without being conceited about it, that she was pretty—at least if the stares she sometimes got from boys meant anything.

"I'm coming too," Isabel stated quickly.

"We're going to feel like idiots, the four of us running off into the woods in a frenzy when they're probably just gossiping or something," Jeff complained.

"Angel? Gossiping?" Kelly laughed.

Jeff looked at her. "You're right. The witch has probably sacrificed Paula to some pagan deity by now. Only kidding, Brian."

"Sure," Brian said grimly, seizing a lantern.

As they left the clearing, Kelly glanced over her shoulder. Chris and Nathan remained by the fire. "Do you think it's a good idea to leave them alone together?"

Jeff gave the pair a quick once-over. "They look calm enough now. If Nathan makes some kind of wisecrack while we're gone, he'll deserve to get wasted."

They followed the path all the way to the outhouse without seeing any sign of Paula or Angel.

"Paula!" Brian called out.

The forest's brooding silence bore down on them

and Kelly doubted his voice carried very far. The trees seemed to muffle sound, shutting off any but the loudest noises after a couple of hundred feet.

"Where could they have gone?" Jeff wondered aloud.

Kelly turned to Isabel. "Can you tell?"

Isabel laughed, shaking her head. "If you mean how am I, noble savage, at tracking through the woods—forget it. I'm a suburban Indian. The only game I stalk is a turkey sandwich now and then. Let's go back to the cabin. They may have just stepped off the trail and we missed them."

Although Isabel's voice was calm, Kelly detected a nervousness in her pretty brown eyes, which seemed unusually animated. Was she worried the two girls might have wandered off the path and stumbled on one of the holes in the ground Porter had warned them about? She didn't know what else it could be, but she couldn't ask her now, while Brian was within earshot. He'd panic.

They were halfway back to the cabin when Isabel held up a hand, stopping them.

"What is it?" Kelly asked. Then she heard it too.

A soft rustle in the leaves, from very close by.

Jeff stiffened beside her, listened for another moment, then stepped out of the glow of Brian's lantern and parted the shadowy branches just off the trail. Angel sat on the ground, surrounded by briars and three-leaved plants that reminded Kelly of poison ivy. *The perfect habitat for her,* Kelly thought wickedly.

But she could tell from Angel's puffy eyes that the girl had been crying, and somehow that moved her.

91

She'd never pictured Angel being vulnerable. Kelly knelt down beside her.

"What's wrong, Angel?"

An angry, stubborn look stole over the girl's powdery white face. "You're all so stupid!" she shouted, jumping up to brush roughly past Kelly. She took off at a run for the cabin.

"What's gotten into her?" Jeff asked.

"I think that's normal, for her," murmured Kelly, sorry she'd wasted her sympathy. She looked around. "I wonder where Paula is?"

"Back at the cabin already," Jeff suggested. "She and Angel must have had a fight. Paula probably went around the long way to avoid her."

Brian scanned the dark woods with concern. "I'd better go look for her."

"Come on back to the cabin, Bri," Kelly begged. "She's probably already there, waiting for you."

"Maybe."

"I'll go with you, Brian," Isabel offered eagerly.

Surprised, Kelly stared at the Indian girl. She was reminded of her wish for Brian, for someone less possessive and bossy than Paula—and Isabel seemed like such a sweet girl. If she was hoping for a chance to flirt with Brian, good luck to her.

Jeff stepped forward as if he'd been propelled by a spring. "I'll walk Kelly back to the cabin. Keep the lantern, Brian. You'll need it more than we will."

"Thanks. If you two find Paula back there, just give a yell." He stepped off of the path, cutting between bushes with Isabel close behind.

Kelly checked the glowing hands of her watch. "It's

after nine-thirty. We're supposed to be inside, lights out at ten. If Porter finds half of us missing—"

"I don't want to think about it," Jeff groaned, already starting to retrace their path back toward the cabin.

The light from Brian's lantern faded to a dim burnt-orange. Kelly reluctantly moved away from its circle of safety. Although she'd desperately wanted to be alone with Jeff, now that she was, she was a little afraid. Something had turned him off to her earlier. Whatever she'd done, she didn't want to repeat. Forgetting to pay attention to where she put her feet in the darkness, she tripped over a root, only just managing to catch herself against a sturdy trunk.

"You okay?" Jeff asked over his shoulder.

"Yeah. No moon tonight. I can't see very well."

"Here," he said, reaching back. His fingertips brushed her shirt-front. "Oh, sorry."

Kelly grasped his hand before he could withdraw it in embarrassment, and they walked on slowly in silence.

At last Jeff spoke, his voice sounding tight. "I should apologize for this afternoon . . . getting you wet."

He had barely splashed her at all. "It was just in fun," she said softly.

"I was worried I might have scared you or something."

"You didn't."

"You screamed." He sounded irritated.

"What was I supposed to do, sing "The Star-Spangled Banner"?"

93

"You might as well have for all the racket you made!" He fell silent and Kelly marched on, seething. "Sorry," he said again before she could think of an adequate comeback, "I've got a lot on my mind."

But she couldn't help thinking to herself: *Oh, Jeff. What could be more important than me?*

Then they stepped into the clearing and were met by a surprise.

Angel sat with her back against a sapling, staring into the fire. Chris had disappeared, but Nathan crouched close beside Angel, holding her hand, whispering to her with a rapturous look in his eyes.

Kelly stopped, pulling Jeff to a halt. "Just thinking of the two of them together gives me the creeps."

"I don't know," Jeff commented philosophically. "Maybe they were meant for each other."

Kelly pulled the quilted edge of her sleeping bag up to her chin, turning over for the hundredth time, squeezing her eyes shut, praying for sleep. The thin warmth from the fire in the lounge had never really reached the bedroom. She'd laid her bag on top of her bed and crawled in, and it had taken forever for her to get warm. Not at all like her cozy pink-and-white room at home. She was also used to having a nightlight, but there was nothing in the girls' room to break the solid cold blackness.

Miraculously, no one had gotten into trouble for traipsing around in the woods after curfew. Although it had been ten-thirty before Isabel and Brian located Paula and returned with her to the cabin, Porter had never come out of his room to check up on them.

Paula had explained that Angel had "gotten weird" on her. When she'd left the other girl and tried to take a shortcut back to the cabin, she'd lost her way.

Kelly turned her head to survey the room, but couldn't make out anything beyond the edge of her own bed. She remembered the layout: Isabel's cot nearest hers, then Paula's. Angel had pulled her bed into the far corner, as if she wanted to be no closer to the other girls than they wanted to be to her.

Kelly had begun to hear Isabel's resonant, even breathing almost immediately after she blew out the lantern's flame. The other two girls were quiet, but she couldn't tell if they were asleep.

"Paula," Kelly whispered, "are you awake?"

No answer, just a small animal sound from the corner—Angel's corner.

Good grief, Kelly fretted. *I'm sleeping in the same room with a certifiable lunatic.*

For a time, she had agreed with Brian—that Angel's eccentricities were likely just attention-getting devices. She'd figured that once the new girl got to know them all a little better, she'd calm down. But if anything, Angel seemed to be getting wilder, and since they had to spend another four days with her in these remote hills, Kelly felt more than a little concerned.

To calm herself, she tried a little positive imaging. Concentrating on thoughts of Jeff—the way his handsome tanned face looked in the firelight, how his strong arms had felt when he'd lifted her and charged off into the woods as if he were a brave knight, rescuing her—his princess!—from . . . from what? A dragon? A clawing wolf? Or some other worse, un-imaginable evil?

Gradually the voices from the boys' room became fainter, then ceased entirely. Kelly felt her eyes grow heavy, close, then there was blessed nothingness and, for a while—a minute, an hour, maybe longer—she floated in dreamless sleep. Sweet marshmallowy blissful sleep.

Something woke her with a start.

Kelly yanked down the zipper on her sleeping bag and sat up on the cot, breathing hard, perspiring through the oversized T-shirt she'd worn to bed, try-ing to fix her sleep-hazed brain on whatever had jolted her out of sound slumber.

A high-pitched scream grabbed her around the heart and held on, seeming to squeeze forever.

"Paula, did you hear that?" she gasped, her pulse hammering. "Isabel?"

No one answered. How could they sleep through *that*? Whoever was doing the screaming hadn't let up, even for a breath.

Leaping out of bed, she somehow found her jeans in the dark on the floor. Pulled them on over her underwear. Crammed her bare feet into already-tied tennis shoes.

Kelly burst into the empty lounge, pausing only a fraction of a second to orient herself. The cry was definitely coming from outside. Should she take time to light a lantern? Yes. She'd be running into trees without one.

Quickly she located matches on the shelf near the door, struck a match with shaking fingers, and slid it under the glass chimney. She grabbed the Coleman, dashed out through the cabin door and across the clearing and . . . headlong into a tall figure.

"What's going on?" she cried. "Oh, Jeff!"

"I heard something . . . a scream." He'd been heading in the opposite direction, up the path from the lake and was breathing raggedly, as if he'd been running a distance. His skin above the neckline of his warm-up suit glistened with a fine layer of sweat, although the temperature outside had dropped considerably since they'd arrived around noon.

"I heard it too," Kelly gasped.

"I think we ought to get—oh, Mr. Porter—"

"Who is making that awful noise?" the teacher demanded, stepping out of the cabin. "Why are you two out of your rooms?"

Jeff started to explain, "We heard something—"

"It sounded like someone calling for help . . . down by the lake," Kelly jumped in breathlessly, aware of the seconds ticking away. "I was on my way to see what had happened when I ran into Jeff."

Porter, in a flannel robe, his plaid-pajama legs and corduroy slippers extending below the hem, looked questioningly at the young wrestling team captain.

"I must have heard it a few seconds sooner," Jeff muttered, avoiding Porter's X-ray glare. "I was just going to investigate when I realized I'd better check with you first, and I . . . I turned back."

Kelly squinted at him. *But you've been running for more than a few seconds.*

While Porter had questioned them, there had been an eerie silence. Now the cry came again, louder, sounding more like a tortured animal than anything human.

"Let me have that," Porter ordered, snatching the lantern from Kelly's hand. "You two go back inside."

He bolted down the path toward the lake. Jeff and Kelly exchanged looks and immediately took off after him.

Jeff easily passed Porter, his cross-country stride long and almost relaxed. Pounding the dirt path behind them, Kelly managed to avoid tricky roots and low branches but fell behind. As Jeff surged ahead, with Porter managing to keep a surprisingly close second with the lantern, Kelly was running almost totally blind.

Cries for help echoed through the trees. "Help! Oh, God, help!"

"Sounds like a girl!" Jeff shouted over his shoulder, and took off on a side path he seemed sure of.

Porter followed. So did Kelly, without thinking of her own safety, drawn on by terror of what they'd find at the source of that bone-piercing cry.

Suddenly, she could hear footsteps coming up behind her. She glanced backward. Isabel appeared out of the gloom, a lantern in one hand.

"Kelly, wait!" she shouted. "Was that you screaming?"

"No . . . come on."

The two girls scrambled down a sandy ledge onto a beach of coarse pebbles. Porter had peeled off his robe and was throwing it over a small, trembling figure.

At first Kelly didn't recognize the girl. Her lovely

blonde hair was darkly wet, dripping and tangled across her face. Her jeans and T-shirt were plastered to her shivering body.

"Paula!" Kelly automatically scanned the shore and spotted a small hut that must have been the boat shed. The door was open. "Where's Brian?" she asked, her heart shooting up into her throat.

Paula was trembling so hard her eyes weren't focusing.

"Where is he, Paula?" She seized the girl's shoulders, shaking them. "Where *is* he?"

"I see something out in the lake!" Jeff shouted. "A rowboat."

Kelly spun around. Jeff was pointing to a low shape on the water, barely visible in the dim orange glow from shore. Later she recalled that Chris and Nathan had appeared at the woods' edge at about that time with a flurry of confused questions. But her brain had quit registering details by then.

"Oh, God, no!" Kelly wailed, releasing Paula and staggering back a step. She felt weak and violently sick to her stomach. "Was Brian with you in the boat? Paula, damn you, *talk* to me!"

Paula kept shaking her head to everything. "No," she mumbled at last. "No. I wasn't in the boat. Not *there*. A stranger . . . it was a stranger." She stammered, her voice rising in hysteria, her eyes wild. "Brian tried to . . . to protect me. It's *all* my fault. Oh!" With a piercing shriek she threw off Porter's robe and would have run back into the water if Nathan and Chris hadn't restrained her. Porter kept trying to get more information out of her, which seemed impossible given her condition.

Isabel stood by silently, gazing at the gently bobbing boat, a sad look of resignation in her dark eyes.

But Kelly had no intention of standing helplessly on the beach. She knew Porter would never give permission for any of his students to go into the water, but she realized that seconds were precious. She had competed on swim teams since she was ten; she was the strongest swimmer in the group at Deep Creek. Paula had tried to help Brian, but failed. Now it was up to her.

Jeff must have had similar thoughts. He started pulling off his Nikes, his gaze grimly latched on the rowboat.

Porter whipped around in time to see him fling his second shoe onto dry sand. "No, Mr. Mitchell!" he bellowed. "Forget it. You couldn't even *see* anything out there. I'm not going to be responsible for losing two students in one night!"

As if one is okay? Kelly thought.

Jeff started arguing with him.

While Porter's back was turned, Kelly stripped off her jeans, leaving her T-shirt and panties on, and dove into the shallows. *Cold! Like ice!*

Her body cut through the numbing, black water. She tried not to think of Brian . . . out there alone . . . how many minutes? How long could he survive submerged in this freezing water?

"Miss Peterson, come back!" Porter shouted as she broke the surface.

She ignored him, ignored the others who shouted

for her to turn around, and lengthened the stroke of her crawl.

Bri! Oh, God, please be all right!

In seconds, she was too far out for anyone to stop her. Praying the rowboat hadn't drifted far from the spot where Brian went in, Kelly swam for it. She pulled herself up over the splintery edge, shaking the water out of her eyes, peered inside, hoping against all odds that he'd managed to drag himself into the boat.

He wasn't there. And her heart swelled with fear, feeling as if it would burst.

"No. No!" she screamed, refusing to give up. "Brian, where are you! Answer me!" Kelly scanned the lake's surface, searching for a shape bobbing on the dark water. Then the most horrible thought of all struck her—the only reason he'd be floating and not answering her was if he was already *dead*.

Down. He *must* be right underneath her.

Bending at the hips, Kelly dove. Almost immediately a chill of pure ice struck her, far colder than the water she'd swum through to reach the boat. A deeper, nerve-deadening chill lurked a few feet below the surface, and she remembered with sudden fear Porter's warning about the treacherous currents of the underground springs and Isabel's story of Gweemush, greedy god of death.

Inch by inch her body succumbed to the bitter water, the cold stiffening her limbs, slowing her breathing, her pulse. Still she forced herself to dive, again and again, coming up with only handfuls of slimy lake grass, sensing there were many more feet of water than she could possibly reach with the air in her lungs.

Each time she rose to the surface, tears trickled down her cheeks, mixing with lake water streaming from her hair. At last, she drew a deep breath and, kicking fiercely, dove far deeper than she'd ever normally dare. Twenty feet below Deep Creek's wavelets. Deeper still. And without warning a fierce, possessive tug yanked at her body.

Gweemush? she thought.

Terrified, she tucked and somersaulted, pointing her head toward the barely visible lantern glow from the shore, kicked and kicked again. The tug grew harder, more determined.

Let go of me! Kelly pleaded.

Fighting for survival, she cut the unyielding water with her arms, kicking like hell, terrified out of her mind—for herself and for dear sweet Brian. After what seemed like forever, she'd made no noticeable progress against the cruel pull from the bottom of the lake, and her lungs were burning, starving for oxygen. Then, miraculously, the water broke over her head in a cold spray and she scrambled, sobbing and coughing and drinking air into her lungs, over the gunwale of the rowboat, into the protection of its lumpy hull—but without her best friend.

Chapter 7

Dawn had colored a crayon-pastel border around the dark horizon by the time the stunned SAT group made their way back to the cabin. Much later, Kelly still couldn't remember anything from the time she'd curled up, shivering and exhausted and defeated, in the bottom of the rowboat to the moment when someone threw a towel over her head and started rubbing.

She sat limply while dripping clothing was peeled off of her, not objecting or even caring although she was normally very modest. Nothing mattered anymore. Brian was gone.

"Do you feel warmer now?" a soft voice asked.

Kelly looked up into anxious eyes. Isabel. The two of them seemed to be alone in the girls' bedroom. Kelly's soggy T-shirt and underwear lay in a heap on the floor. The scratchy wool blanket next to her skin was warming, but it also brought back unwelcome sensation. And memory.

Oh, God, today's Thanksgiving Day! Brian died on Thanksgiving Day!

"Where's Paula?" Kelly asked thickly, her lips the last to thaw out.

"In the lounge. The boys are looking after her until

Porter gets back. He's still down at the lake. Jeff's making coffee. Do you want some?"

Gallons. A flood of it to drown in, Kelly thought morbidly.

"Yes," she murmured.

"I'll bring you a cup." Isabel straightened up.

"No!" Kelly grabbed the girl's arm urgently. "I want to be with the others."

The feeling had struck her without reason—the need to be in the middle of a lot of people. For safety? To count heads too. Why she should feel this way she wasn't sure. Possibly because she was afraid that someone else might turn up missing. Or maybe it was an instinctive knowledge that it was important she account for everyone's whereabouts right now and during the previous hours.

"I'll get dressed," she murmured, her voice still weak, quavering.

Isabel shook her head firmly. "You should climb into your sleeping bag, get warm. There's nothing you can do. Nothing anyone can do until it gets light."

However, Kelly insisted, "I want to talk to Paula. I have to know what happened."

Isabel sighed. "You were only half conscious all the way back from the lake. I guess you didn't hear."

"Hear what?"

"About the guy who attacked Brian."

"I heard Paula babbling something about a stranger, down by the lake."

"A man," Isabel said hesitantly. "It's hard to know exactly what happened from the way she was rambling on. She's in shock, I expect. I can't believe he really . . ." She shook her head vaguely, biting her lower lip.

Kelly pulled a pair of sweats from beneath her bed and slid them on.

"I don't know why you want to go out there now," Isabel persisted. "You need to rest."

Kelly grabbed her brush from the windowsill, dragged it carelessly through the tangles of wet, red hair around her face. "We have to get as much information as we can from Paula—right away, before she shuts the details out of her mind. The police will need everything they can get to track down this guy."

"Maybe you'd better let them ask her," Isabel suggested gently.

Kelly looked at her. "When do you think they'll get here?"

Isabel frowned, puzzled. "As soon as Porter calls— Oh, no. That's right, no telephone."

"And he said that we're at least ten miles from the nearest neighbors." Kelly pushed past Isabel, into the lounge.

Chris looked up as Kelly walked in, his big frame casting a shadow in the lantern light that almost filled the room.

"You all right?" he asked gruffly. He sounded angry, and she couldn't help wondering who the emotion was directed at. Her? Brian, for causing all the fuss? The violent outsider?

"I'll be okay," she murmured, her eyes shifting away from his wide face, seeking out Paula.

The delicate blonde was huddled on the couch by

the front window, a blanket around her shoulders, hair still wet and clinging to ivory cheeks, knees drawn up to her tiny chin. Paula stared blankly toward the lake, shivering uncontrollably.

"She won't let anyone touch her," Jeff said, handing Kelly a cup of coffee. "She's gonna catch pneumonia if she doesn't get those wet things off."

Kelly nodded, approaching Paula. The girl must be desperate with worry, not knowing if Brian was dead or alive. Beyond grief. Her entire future might have been destroyed in less than an hour. She looked like a fragment of a person, sitting there alone, and Kelly realized how infrequently she'd seen Paula Schultz without Brian Lopez at her side.

"There's nothing you can do," Kelly whispered, echoing Isabel, her voice feeling all angles in her throat.

Paula didn't even blink.

"Have a sip of my coffee," Kelly offered. When Paula didn't respond, Kelly raised the cup to the girl's lips, making her drink a little. "Better?"

Sure. A little coffee will make everything just rosy, you jerk, a little voice inside Kelly taunted.

But she had to pretend for Paula's sake, didn't she? "Come on, let's get some dry clothes on you." Kelly put down her cup, and tried prying Paula off the wet patch of couch.

The girl didn't fight her, but she was dead weight, immovable.

Nathan stepped closer. Bending to peer into Paula's eyes, he waved a hand in front of them. Paula didn't

106

even blink. "She's a zombie," he declared. "Probably don't feel a thing."

"Shut up!" Kelly snapped.

"Hey," Nathan objected, "chill out. I was just trying to help."

"Back off," Jeff ordered in a low voice, moving between Kelly and the biker. His eyes had a dangerous look Kelly had seen him aim at an opponent, just before he pinned him to the wrestling mat.

Nathan raised both hands in a gesture of innocence. "It's cool, man."

Kelly shot Jeff a grateful look then turned back toward Paula. "Tell us what happened. You said you had reached the lake. Were you supposed to meet Brian? Were you two planning to take out the boat?"

A soft, almost peaceful smile lifted the corners of Paula's ghastly purple lips. "We were going to glide out across the beautiful lake in the moonlight."

Kelly shook her head, confused. "But Brian was already in the rowboat . . . in the middle of the lake when you got there?"

"He left without me. I changed my mind, but he wouldn't listen."

Something tightened in Kelly's throat. "Listen to what? You said he was already gone?"

Paula's eyes clouded over, looking disoriented. She lowered her head into her hands with a little moan.

Jeff stepped up behind Kelly. "Maybe you should leave her alone . . . she's been through hell tonight."

"No!" Kelly snapped, her green eyes afire with new hope. "We have to find out exactly what happened. If she's so mixed up, maybe she just *thinks*

Brian drowned. Maybe he swam to shore, and he's hurting and can't get back here or call to us or . . . Oh, God, he *can't* be dead!'' Kelly broke into hiccupping sobs.

Jeff's arms came around her, and she smothered her tears against his neck. He smelled like pond weeds, and she suddenly knew how she'd gotten from the boat to the cabin. He must have swum out for her, pulled or rowed the boat to shore with her in it. Then someone—Jeff again—had carried her here, in her wet underwear.

Blushing, she opened her eyes and looked up at him.

''I don't think Paula could have seen enough of this guy or their fight to describe it,'' Jeff said. ''Not from the shore, in the dark.''

Kelly slid out of his arms. ''But where did he go? The boat was still there.''

''Maybe there was a second boat,'' Isabel suggested.

''Yeah,'' Chris said slowly, ''Brian was going to take out the rowboat earlier, like for a test run. But he didn't. So maybe he got to the boat house before Paula and took it out by himself, then—''

''Then some creep came along in another boat and attacked him,'' Nathan finished.

''Why would anyone do that?'' Kelly demanded.

Jeff shrugged.

Kelly turned back to Paula. ''Was there a second boat?'' Paula's face stayed buried in her palms. ''Or was the stranger in the rowboat with him?''

''Talk about not making any sense,'' Nathan interrupted. "Why would Brian go off for a cruise around the lake with some guy? Unless—" He leered suggestively. "He wasn't AC/DC, was he?"

Kelly glared at him. "Shut up, zit."

"Nathan and you are right about one thing," Jeff mused, rubbing his temple as if he had a headache. "None of this makes any sense. There were life jackets in the boat shed. Brian left them behind, which was a dumb move."

Kelly whirled to face the tall, athletic senior. "What are you saying? That he *deserved* to drown because he broke a rule?"

"As it turns out," Jeff retorted, "if he'd followed the rule, he might be alive now."

Kelly's face flushed with anger. What was wrong with everyone? It was as if they didn't really *want* to find out the truth!

"I . . . I tried to save him," a voice squeaked apologetically.

Kelly stared into Paula's tear-filled blue eyes. "You swam out from the beach?"

"Y-yes."

"What happened to the stranger?"

"G-o-o-one," Paula moaned. "Nobody was there by the time I reached the boat."

"But that must have only taken a minute, two at the most. Why weren't you able to find Brian and pull him back into the boat?" Kelly knew she was losing it. She shouldn't be blaming poor Paula, of all people. But she felt driven to get at the truth. "Brian could have at least treaded water until you reached him—if he was conscious."

Paula blinked at her, appearing to sink deeper into the couch cushions, tears spilling down her cheeks. "The lake. I couldn't, Kelly. I tried . . . I touched him . . . lost . . . gone—"

Just then the cabin door swung open, and all eyes turned toward it. Angel walked in.

For a long moment, nobody moved or said a word. Then Chris slowly stood up from the table, glowering at Angel. "Where you been, girl?"

Yes. Where? Kelly wondered.

The girls' bedroom had been dark. There was no way of knowing who had still been in bed, who was missing. In fact, Kelly hadn't realized that Paula was gone until they'd found her at the lake.

And what about the boys? Had all of them, with the exception of Brian, been asleep?

No! The answer hit Kelly in the stomach like a clenched fist. She'd run into Jeff in the clearing just outside the cabin, and Chris and Nathan had arrived at the lake several minutes later. Either of them could have come from the cabin or another direction. But she hadn't seen Angel at all during the attempted rescue.

"Where *have* you been, Angel?" Kelly repeated in a flat voice.

Angel's glance swerved slowly, darkly, to fix on Paula.

Kelly felt her insides turn to jelly. How many times in the last twenty-four hours had she wondered about Angel's emotional balance? Yet, somehow, she'd never really believed she would hurt any of them—that she was capable of anything as extreme as *murder*. Anyway, why would she try to hurt Brian? She didn't even know—

Angel's mysterious words replayed in Kelly's mind: *I know you from another life.*

Kelly stared at her. "You witch!" she hissed between gritted teeth. "If you hurt Brian—"

Isabel's hand gently wrapped around Kelly's wrist, restraining her. "We can't start suspecting each other. None of us is a killer."

"How do you know that?" Nathan asked, lounging against the boys' door. "I mean . . . I myself am sort of curious. It's not like I know any of you sports real well."

"Stow it," Jeff advised tightly.

Chris stepped forward bashfully, his eyes meeting Kelly's. "What if he's right? How much does any of us know about the others? Maybe one of us *would* become violent, even kill . . . if he had to. If he couldn't help himself." His face looked more troubled than Kelly had ever seen it.

"What are you talking about?" Jeff demanded.

"I don't know." Chris suddenly looked bewildered and frightened.

"I know what he's talking about," Nathan announced, crossing his arms over his chest as if he was pleased with himself. "Say a guy gets so PO'd he can't control himself, and he pops off and does something he's sorry for later. Know anyone like that, big boy?" he asked nastily.

"Nathan, quit it!" Kelly warned. Standing closer to Chris, she could see the fury rising in his eyes.

But Nathan apparently didn't, and he continued in

111

a grand manner, "Geez, Kelly, you're practically accusing Angel of snuffing your friend, and all the time here's this out-of-control monster hulking around, beating up people right and left. Even *he* is beginning to worry what he might do next! Isn't it obvious he finally went too freakin' far?"

Chris lunged around Jeff, trying to reach Nathan, but the other boy had learned his lesson and deftly stepped behind Kelly, using her as a screen.

"Stop!" Kelly shouted, stomping her foot.

"I'm going to prove you attacked Brian," Nathan taunted Chris. "I won't quit looking until I find *proof!*"

Paula was staring at Nathan, a strange expression in her eyes, as if she couldn't quite comprehend what he was saying—just as Porter came through the front door.

There was instantaneous silence as the teacher observed each of them, his face a calm mask. Beneath it, however, the actress in Kelly was sure she saw traces of another powerful emotion, something he was working hard at controlling.

"Did you find him?" Kelly asked over a painful lump in her throat.

Porter shook his head. "Is everyone but Brian here?" he asked bluntly.

They all nodded.

"I thought I caught a glimpse of someone down by the lake, just as I finished looking around and was ready to head back this way."

"Angel only showed up a minute ago," Jeff volunteered.

Porter studied the girl in the black cape. As if reading a thought that had raced through Kelly's mind a moment earlier, he reached out and touched her sleeve.

It's dry, Kelly guessed. You could tell by looking closely at the cloth. However, Angel could have taken it off.

But what about her hair? Considering its cropped, wild style and the brisk wind across the lake, the black spikes might have dried looking more or less normal.

"All right," Porter said over a long exhalation. "It's only five o'clock in the morning. I want everyone to go back to bed, get a couple hours' sleep."

The lump in Kelly's throat grew still larger. "I can't sleep," she croaked. "I know I can't." *I'll dream of Brian . . . drowning.*

"I want you to try," Porter said firmly, his expression not unkind. "When it's completely light, we'll search the inlets around the lake and the nearby land on the off-chance Brian made it to shore and was too exhausted to find his way back here."

"Why can't we do that now?" Kelly begged.

"Because we have to be alert and we need as much light as possible. Besides, if whoever attacked Brian—"

"You think the guy might still be around?" Jeff broke in.

"No," Porter admitted after only a brief hesitation. "If I believed there was any real chance of that, I wouldn't let any of you leave this cabin. As it is, we'll stay close together, just in case."

"What if we don't find Brian?" Isabel asked softly, casting a concerned look at Paula.

"Whether or not we locate him, we need to notify the police of the attack and reach the bus company so they can send someone to pick us up as soon as possible."

"Call the bus company?" Nathan let out a coarse laugh. "How do we do that, since we're freakin' *cut off from civilization?*"

Porter glared at him. "I'll go for help," he said shortly. "If I start walking around noon, I should reach the nearest occupied houses well before dark. Even if they don't have a phone, they'll have some kind of vehicle. I'll get a ride into town."

"I'll go with you," Nathan offered—probably because Chris was still eyeing him as if he were an irritating insect, calculating when to squash him.

"You'll wait here with the others," Porter ordered.

"But I—"

"I said, you'll stay here until I return with the police. I want all of you in one place, watching out for each other. Now, everyone try to rest until daylight."

Angel retrieved her diary from the folds of her cloak and stared at it as the lounge emptied. Then she sat down in the middle of the floor right where she'd been standing, opened the black velvet-covered book, and read the words she'd only just finished writing:

None of us will leave this place alive.

Reading them under her breath a second time, she decided they had a nice dramatic ring. But that sort of thing no longer seemed so entertaining. She shut the book with an air of finality.

When Angel's parents had told her they'd be sending her on this retreat with a bunch of kids from another school, she'd been upset. Of course she hadn't told them, or her shrink, that it bothered her. That would be normal. She despised "normal."

All of her life she'd wanted to do and be something special. Not a teacher, or bank clerk, or even a procurement specialist for the federal government like her mother. She wanted to see her name in a newspaper headline, be on TV, maybe even get a role in a movie. Somehow grab people's attention and say: *Hey! Here I am. Me!*

There were times she thought it wouldn't matter how she did it—just as long as it happened.

"Hey, what are you doing?"

Angel looked up. It was the boy they called Nathan. He was one of the more interesting students here. He didn't dress or talk or act like the others—or like her—gag—yuppie parents. And he'd been kind to her when Paula had made her cry.

"Writing," she said.

"I saw you doing it on the bus, and last night before lights out."

"I write down everything I see or think," she explained, only afterwards realizing this sounded like too normal a conversation.

"Everything?" Nathan asked with interest. "Lemme see."

She hauled the diary into the shelter of her long, thin arms. "No. It's private."

He shrugged. "Secret stuff, huh? I can dig that. I have a couple of secrets of my own."

She couldn't hide her curiosity. "You do?"

"Sure thing, baby. A whopper."

She thought for a moment. "Does it have anything to do with what happened to that boy last night?"

He considered. "It might. It just might—you never know. Maybe if you let me read your thoughts . . ."

She gripped the book even tighter. The shrink had wanted to see her book too. "No!" she said loudly.

"No big deal. Maybe some other time. I'll show you something anyway." Casting a cautious look at the bedroom doors as if reassuring himself no one would interrupt them, Nathan sat down beside Angel on the floor. "Looky here," he said, pulling his jacket away from his scrawny body, as if flashing a selection of black-market watches.

Angel glimpsed something slender and silver before he covered it again, patting the jacket back into place with satisfaction.

"You took Isabel's knife?" she whispered.

"That's *one* secret. Still don't want to show me what you wrote in your little book?"

She shook her head, ran her tongue over her lip. "You attacked Brian?"

"Man, no way! You kidding? This is just for protection. Listen—" He leaned within inches of her dangling earring, which was shaped like a coiled viper. "Know what I think? Someone iced the rich dude. And I know who done it. This blade is my life insurance."

Angel studied him suspiciously. "You're afraid that someone might kill you to keep you quiet?"

"You should be too. The guy's out of control. Without any warning, he could kill again."

She stared at him, knowing he was either lying or had simply misconstrued whatever evidence he believed he had. Because she knew the truth.

Apparently, he took her silence for a sign of fear. "Hey, don't get shook. It's all right. Old Nathan will look after you. You just stick by me."

"All right," she said sweetly. "I will."

Paula and Isabel were the only ones who remained at the cabin during the morning search. Porter decided Paula wasn't emotionally or physically up to the task—which as time went on was more likely to produce a corpse than a live Brian. As it was, exhaustion had finally overcome her and she dropped off to sleep on her bed. Isabel sat in the lounge, reading, just in case Paula woke before the others returned. Porter didn't think Brian's girlfriend should be left alone.

The teacher had assigned Jeff and Chris to search the neighboring inlet where the old country club—presently boarded up for the winter—was located. Just after the other groups had left to scour their own quadrants, the football player had mumbled a few words about having to go back for something he'd left behind.

"Forgot the lantern," Chris explained when he came out a couple minutes later, holding a Coleman.

Jeff looked at him, surprised, because Chris really wasn't a stupid person. Jeff would have fallen down laughing if anyone else had pulled such a dumb stunt, but he had a healthy respect for Chris's size and temper, an even healthier respect than yesterday. Nathan's accusations had him worried, despite his doubt that Chris would take the trouble to drown anyone when he could much more easily crush him. Still, there was a likable innocence about the guy at times.

"Geez, Chris, it's daylight!" he said mildly. "What do we need that for?"

"It gets dark early this time of year. I thought we might still be out searching late in the afternoon."

"Porter said he'd leave about lunchtime, remember?"

"Oh, yeah." The football player shrugged, looking a little embarrassed as they started down the path toward the lake. "Guess I should take it back."

"Naw. It might come in handy if we fell down one of those holes Porter warned us about. Even though they're supposed to be clearly marked, they could be a hazard. See?"

He pointed out a stone several feet to the right of the path, painted with a red arrow. Walking over, Jeff bent down, dug his fingers among the dead leaves, pine needles, and undergrowth. A hole nearly a foot across appeared.

"How deep is it?" Chris asked.

"I don't know." Jeff grabbed a rotted branch from the ground and probed the hole. "Three feet or so; I can feel the bottom."

"A little kid could fall in there," Chris observed with a frown. "No one would ever find him."

"It's possible. That's why they're marked." Jeff

stood up, intentionally leaving the hole open, making sure the marker was free of leaves.''

The golden morning sun warmed her eyelids. Paula lazily opened them. For a fraction of a second, she smiled—then she remembered the horror of the night before. Brian. Oh, God!

Paula swung her bare legs over the side of the bed. She was wearing her Bryan Adams nightshirt. She had no idea how she'd gotten it on. Only dizzy snatches of memory from the night before were beginning to steal back into her consciousness: Kelly . . . and that exotic-looking Indian girl helping her into bed. Disjointed phrases coming to her as if from a great distance: *I'll go for help*. *Nearest houses before dark.*

Help? No one could help Brian now—at the bottom of a goddamn lake.

Steadying herself with one hand against the wall, Paula stared at the black cloth satchel under Angel's bed, then at the window behind Kelly's cot. She tiptoed to the bedroom door and peaked out into the lounge. Only Isabel was there, reading a magazine, her recorder earphones clipped over her head, her back turned to the door.

Carefully, silently, Paula closed the door again. If she got dressed and slipped out through the window, Isabel probably wouldn't realize she'd gone.

Kelly, Nathan, and Angel searched the marshy reeds around the inlet running east of the cabin. Actually, Nathan and Kelly did the searching. Angel was pretty much useless. She spent most of the time chasing chipmunks, creatures she seemed to find fascinating. When she couldn't catch any, she climbed a tree and looked down on the others as they did all the work.

Before going to the inlet, Kelly had insisted they visit the boat shed. Something had been nagging at her subconscious as she lay awake on her cot, something disturbing that she couldn't explain. She remembered pulling herself into the rowboat, shivering, grieving for Brian, then she'd collapsed into the bottom of the boat . . . and it had felt . . . lumpy. Why did the word "lumpy" occur to her? Not slimy, or cold, or hard. Lumpy.

In the dim boat house, she climbed into the little boat and felt around on the bottom with her hand. The wood was still damp. Ridges that formed the skeleton of the craft crossed the hull.

"Did you lose something?" Nathan asked.

"No." She sighed, puzzled. "It's nothing, I guess. Let's go." But she couldn't shake the feeling that she'd missed something important.

Now they'd spent nearly an hour searching through waist-deep swamp grass.

"This is not the place to look for him," Angel announced from her perch.

Breathing hard, Kelly propped her knuckles on her hips and glared up at the girl. "You saw something last night, didn't you?"

Angel pressed her lips together, refusing to answer.

Maybe she was as sinister as she pretended. However, Kelly noticed that the teasing twinkle so obvious the day before in Angel's heavily mascaraed eyes was no longer evident. For a second the girl's glance dropped, met Kelly's, then she shot a speculative look at Nathan as if afraid of saying anything in front of him. Had Nathan's vow to dig up proof against Chris intimidated her? Or was there some other reason she was afraid of him?

"Nathan," Kelly suggested, "why don't you give that cove just past the boat rental docks a quick look. I'll help Angel down from the tree and be right over."

Nathan grinned at her, winked, and moved off. "Fine by me, sweet cakes."

Kelly rolled her eyes and turned back to Angel's tree. "I don't know what makes you tick," she whispered. "But if you laid even a finger on Brian, if you had *anything* to do with—"

"I warned her," Angel said woodenly, talking to her skull necklace.

Kelly scowled, wondering how much of what the girl said should be taken seriously. "Warned who?"

"Paula."

Kelly's stomach tightened reflexively. Had there been a romantic connection between Angel and Brian that no one knew about? That seemed unthinkable. Could Brian ever be attracted to someone as spaced-out as Angel? Although . . . when Kelly looked closely—mentally discarding the atrocious costume, chalky white makeup, and thickly drawn lines of kohl around her eyes—she could see the makings of an attractive, perhaps even dramatically appealing girl. However, she doubted Brian would start up a serious relationship, or even a semi-serious fling, without telling her. Kelly and Brian had shared their most intimate secrets and feelings for so very long. Their friendship had been precious indeed. And now, a tear slid down her cheek as she looked up into this goddamn tree wishing Angel would let her in on her secrets.

"What did you warn Paula about?" Kelly asked, keeping her voice low just in case Nathan might be lurking nearby, hidden among the reeds.

"The danger of . . . of the lake."

"I don't understand," Kelly said, trying to be patient.

Angel didn't answer.

"What about this stranger . . . Brian's killer? You were wandering around in the dark last night, weren't you? Did you see him?"

Angel gazed down at her. "There was no stranger."

"You mean you didn't see him?"

Angel shook her head, her voice immediately switching to a low, ceremonial drone. "We know . . . each of us, and yet . . . we know nothing. There are no strangers among us."

Oh, damn, Kelly thought. *No strangers . . . And we are all brothers and sisters in this world. If Angel wasn't a loony tune, she must be some kind of religious freak!*

But the question most on Kelly's mind was not what Angel was but what she was capable of doing. Almost at once another idea occurred to her that soured her stomach.

"You saw no strangers," Kelly repeated, carefully

watching Angel's expression, "but . . ." Dare she ask? ". . . but did you see anyone else? Anyone in our group besides Paula and Brian?"

Angel wrinkled her nose as if she smelled something distasteful. "I know him."

Trying to understand Angel was so totally exasperating! Kelly had to fill in three missing sentences between each question and the girl's answers.

"You know him," Kelly repeated carefully, wanting to be sure she didn't read anything into Angel's statements that wasn't meant to be there. *"He* is one of us . . . the person you saw?"

Angel gave a sharp nod, then looked directly down at Kelly from her limb.

"The name," Kelly begged hoarsely. *"Just tell me the name!"*

"Jeffrey," whispered Angel. And Kelly's heart broke in two.

Chapter 8

Someone had relit the campfire and it was blazing merrily. Jeff brought his lunch outside to eat. He sat alone under a tall, long-needled pine, mechanically shoving food into his mouth. It tasted like cardboard.

Kelly had avoided him ever since they'd returned to the cabin from a fruitless search—no Brian, no body— only a felt fabric letter T Nathan had scooped out of the reeds. Jeff was hurt and confused by Kelly's rejection, and finally couldn't stand to look at the back of her lovely red head any longer.

The cabin door swung open, and for a second he hoped it was she, coming out to explain why she was ticked off at him. Nathan appeared, greasy potato chips heaped high on a paper plate.

"Jeffy, my boy," he crowed with forced cheer.

Jeff raised a hand in limp welcome. He felt sorry for Nathan. No one wanted to be his friend. On the other hand, Nathan didn't work very hard at winning people over. He smelled bad much of the time, was obnoxious, and now his bloodshot eyes led Jeff to think he'd smuggled in a supply of liquor.

Nathan sat down beside him and crunched on his chips.

"Were you and Brian best buddies or something?" he asked, his voice slurring just a little.

"No."

"You been so quiet. I thought maybe—"

"No," Jeff said shortly, "I hardly knew him."

He didn't really want to talk. Kelly was on his mind, and he couldn't stop thinking about how coldly she was treating him.

Perhaps it had finally hit her that her friend might be gone, forever. If Brian was really dead, he could wait until her grief became bearable, until she opened up to him again. Or maybe she was still mad because of what he'd said earlier about Brian and the life jackets.

He tried to put her out of his mind and concentrate on Brian's mysterious death. The possibility of there being another boat occurred to him again. That second boat was what he'd been looking for as he and Chris slogged through the marsh grass and tramped the stony beach, then jogged around a couple more coves. He'd been searching for a place where someone might have dragged a boat up out of the water. Actually he'd located two little flat-bottom fishing skiffs, but their wood was completely dry: weeds and grass had grown up around them. They obviously hadn't been moved since the end of the summer.

So, there had been *one* boat. Which meant Brian had been in it with a stranger—just as bad as climbing into a car with someone you didn't know. What could have compelled the guy to do that? Unless— Unless he knew and trusted the person. Still, that didn't mean it had to be someone in the group.

"Thought all you rich dudes stuck together," Nathan broke in on his thoughts. "That's why I figured you knew him."

Something inside Jeff set off a warning bell. He squinted at Nathan. "You didn't like Brian," he guessed.

"I didn't say that." Stuffing a fistful of chips into his mouth, Nathan spoke through the crunching. "Wish my old man was the generous type, that's all."

"What do you mean by that?"

Nathan laughed, his reddened eyes watering. "Everyone *knows* Lopez Realty paid for the dude's ticket into the Air Force Academy."

"Where did you hear that?"

"Around," Nathan muttered evasively.

"It's not true. He was a good student—he earned his spot."

"Yeah, sure."

Jeff didn't like the turn of conversation. He was seeing a hidden hostility in Nathan he either hadn't known existed or hadn't taken seriously before now. "What did you really have against Brian Lopez?"

Nathan shook his head. "Look, it's no big deal. I just can't stomach guys who have it so easy they don't know what it's like to work for a buck. Lopez's crowd hung out at the theater a lot. They'd have dinner at the Surf and Turf first, come to a show, then take off together for Friendly's or someplace for dessert."

"So?" Jeff had done that dozens of times. Sometimes he saw Brian and his friends, sometimes not. He hadn't paid much attention at the time—it was a Friday-night ritual.

"I keep forgetting, you're just like him," Nathan grumbled darkly, his eyes shifting behind his shades. "What's it run you for a night, with a date? Forty bucks? More? That's half my week's freakin' salary. You guys make me wanna puke! A night out don't make a dent in your allowance. You're always flashing a wad of bills. But for me, that's a hell of a lot of money. I never got more than a couple of bucks on me at a time."

Jeff winced. He had about seventy-five dollars in his pocket right now, and he didn't even need it. Just force of habit.

Nathan pushed up off the ground, tossing the rest of his chips and paper plate into the fire. "It was a mistake coming here . . . thinking I could turn my life around in just five days . . . letting you talk me into staying in the same woods with that j—" He stopped abruptly, his watery eyes clouding over. "I gotta go."

Jeff jumped up. "Wait. What were about to say? Something about Chris, right?"

"Hey man, I ain't diggin' my own grave by opening my trap any more now. Just wait till the cops show," Nathan promised with a lopsided grin. "I got *plenty* of sweet stuff to tell them about this little group."

Jeff considered Nathan's retreating back, then sat down on the cold ground again. The booze talking— it had to be. He shook his head. When he looked up again a redheaded vision was standing over him.

* * *

Kelly took a deep breath. A moment ago she'd made up her mind to confront Jeff, to demand that he tell her why he'd lied to Porter last night, tell her where he'd been, what part he'd played in Brian's disappearance. Not knowing was driving her crazy! But as soon as she gazed down into his troubled blue eyes, her mouth dried up and refused to work.

"I'm sorry about what I said . . . you know, about Brian," Jeff mumbled after an uneasy moment.

She gazed at the fire, watching Nathan's paper plate shrink and blacken. Deeper down in the orange embers, ebony curls of ash glowed, still recognizable as sheets of paper, and for a second she thought it strange that someone had used paper for kindling when there were so many dry twigs around.

"I said, I'm sorry, Kelly."

She forced her lips into clumsy action. "That's . . . all right."

"You don't sound as if you really believe it was all right."

Kelly looked at Jeff. "I Just don't think it's nice to talk about someone who died, as if were their fault."

"I didn't mean it that way."

She swallowed, blinked away the moisture forming beneath her lids before it could form teardrops. "I don't suppose you did."

Jeff looked off through the trees toward the lake. He was being a gentleman, pretending he didn't notice she was crying, and she appreciated the gesture.

"Do you think the police will find the guy who did it?" Jeff finally asked.

Kelly glared at him. "They'll find the bastard."

Jeff nodded—unaware of the fact she included him at the top of her list of suspects—then stood up in front of her. He was head and shoulders taller than she, and his short, dark hair curled softly at one corner of his forehead in a way that made her want to smooth it out with her fingertips—just to watch it snap back into that adorable little curlicue again. For a long minute their eyes locked. Kelly stopped breathing, her pulse growing loud in her ears, a pleasant dizziness stealing over her. She had a vision of her and Jeff strolling across a sunlit field, hand in hand.

"Want to go for a walk?" Jeff whispered.

The field of her imagination turned into murky woods. And the wolf of her nightmare slowly merged with Jeff's body. Kelly became his willing victim . . .

With an effort Kelly shook off the dangerous spell Jeff had woven around her. She glanced nervously back at the cabin.

"No," she said regretfully, "I think . . . I think we'd better stay here."

But instead he moved closer, so close she could feel his warm breath tickling her cheek. "If it makes you feel any better, I don't believe there was anyone around here last night, except for us."

Kelly gave him a sharp look. "Are you saying . . . one of *us* killed Brian?"

He shrugged. "It's the most likely scenario."

"That's supposed to make me feel better?"

"If you honestly want the truth, you have to accept all eventualities."

"I can live with the truth. Can *you?*" she demanded bluntly, beginning to turn away before the words had left her lips.

Jeff reached out and grabbed her wrists, forcing her to face him again. "What do you mean by that?"

"Let go of me!"

"I'm holding on for a reason. Enough hints, Kelly. What have you been conjuring up in that crazy red head? Tell me, then maybe I'll let you go."

She pulled hard against his grip, but he didn't release her. "Fine," she gasped. "I'll tell you what's on my mind. You were running *toward* the cabin, *away* from Paula's screams."

"I told you why. I'd come back for Porter."

"It was a lie!" she accused. "Porter was too upset to notice, but you were streaming with sweat and it was a freezing cold night. You must have been out here for a lot longer than you admitted to him, and you were doing something physical to work up all that sweat. Did you and Brian have a fight?"

Jeff slowly released her wrists, looking away.

Tell me! she pleaded silently. *Give me some logical reason for all of this!*

"Angel saw you down by the lake." There, she'd said it, now the ball was in his court. He had to explain himself.

Jeff stared at her in horror. "What did she claim she saw?"

"She didn't elaborate," Kelly said dryly. "It was difficult enough to pry a name out of her."

He nodded, looking somewhat relieved, then gave Kelly a shy look. "I was running."

"Running from what?"

"Not running to or from anything. Working off nervous energy. I couldn't sleep. There's this girl, and she's . . . " He scuffed his heels in the dirt. "Well, she's been on my mind a lot lately and—"

"I see," Kelly cut him off. She was embarrassed and disappointed. Without another word she headed for the cabin door. If there was one thing she didn't want to hear right now it was Jeff Mitchell gushing over some ditzy girl.

Porter packed a sandwich and canister of drinking water in a knapsack. He stood at the doorway of the cabin, wearing nattily pressed chinos, a suede jacket, and Irish wool cap. Kelly thought he looked more like a model for *GQ* than a man setting out on a hike through the woods.

"How long will you be gone?" she asked anxiously.

"Three, maybe four hours at most."

"Sure you don't want me to go with you, Mr. P.?" Nathan offered.

"I'll be fine," the teacher said solemnly, giving each of the group a last critical once-over. "All of you stay right here until I return with the police. I'll be back before you know it."

At the time, nobody doubted his word.

"What's taking him so long?" Paula wailed. She paused from pacing the cabin floor long enough to dig a pretzel out of a plastic bag and crunch absently on it.

Jeff sat on the couch, earphones on, listening with concentration to a tape. Chris was on his eighth set of push-ups. Nathan and Angel had cuddled up together on the floor in front of the fire, his arm around her. Isabel was in the bedroom, packing, the last one to do so.

"Maybe he had trouble finding anyone home or flagging down someone on the highway," Kelly suggested, not really sure she believed her own excuse after all this time.

It was seven o'clock and dark; the kids hadn't bothered starting dinner because they were convinced Porter would show up any minute. However, he'd left almost six hours earlier, and they hadn't heard from him or the police yet.

Kelly glanced worriedly at Paula, still wearing a path across the braided rug. She was becoming increasingly distraught. It was becoming more and more unlikely that Brian could have survived last night's incident. Paula still hadn't eaten anything more substantial than a couple of pretzels, and she'd spent most of the day napping in her room—oblivion being preferable to a conscious state, no doubt.

Isabel stepped into the lounge, a grim expression on her face. "Who took it?" she demanded, her face white, eyes many shades darker than normal.

"Who took what?" Kelly asked.

"My knife. I brought a hunting knife; it was in my suitcase. Now it's gone."

"Forty-two, forty-three, forty-four," Chris continued counting, now performing impressive one-handed push-ups.

Paula stopped pacing and stared at Isabel. "Why would you bring a knife?"

132

"Are you sure it didn't fall down between your clothes?" Kelly asked before Isabel could answer.

"I checked everywhere—even in the other suitcases in the room," she said, looking directly at Angel. "Do you always take dead frogs with you on trips?"

"They're much easier to transport than live ones," Angel answered with indisputable logic.

Isabel groaned. "Well, *someone* took my grandfather's knife. I want it back right now." She held out a hand.

No one moved, said a word, or—Kelly was sure—breathed. Except for Chris who was closing in on sixty-eight.

"Fine," Isabel said briskly, "I'll search the boys' room then."

Chris looked up from the floor where he'd stopped in the middle of his set of push-ups, breathing heavily from exertion, a faint trail of sweat across his forehead. He frowned at Isabel's departing back. "Where's she going?"

"To look through our stuff," Jeff answered in a bored tone. "She's got it into her head that one of us took something."

In the next second, all hell broke loose.

Teeth clenched, Chris launched himself with a wall-shaking snarl at the bedroom door. The change had come over Chris so quickly, like a sudden summer squall, sunshine to monsoon in a moment, unlike any mood swing Kelly had ever witnessed.

Recognizing the crazed look in his eyes she'd seen on the football field and just yesterday when he'd nearly strangled Nathan, she leaped to her feet and took off after him. Jeff wasn't far behind.

As luck would have it, Isabel had gone directly to Chris's duffel bag. She was pulling out jockstraps and Fruit of the Looms by the fistful when he grabbed her by her long, gleaming hair, yanking her off her feet.

"Ouch!" she shrieked, swinging at him with her closed left fist while still clenching a couple of sweatshirts in her right. "Lemme go!" She struck him forcefully in the belly; he didn't flinch.

Kelly charged at Chris, pounding him on the back, screaming. "Chris! *Stop* it!"

But he didn't seem to hear her. "You leave my stuff alone!" he bellowed at Isabel, shaking her until her teeth chattered. "You hear me?"

Jeff pulled Kelly aside and reached up from behind Chris. He latched his forearm in a cross-face hold around Chris's head. It was a brutal wrestling move he'd used to win regionals last year, but Kelly knew that he had to do something drastic to force Chris to release Isabel.

Unfortunately, he was outweighed by at least forty pounds, and his efforts only seemed to further enrage Chris, who shook poor Isabel until tears sprang from her eyes.

"Nathan, *do* something!" Kelly shrieked.

The skinny boy stood in the middle of the room, pressing his hand to his chest, an indecisive expression on his face as if he was trying to make up his mind about something.

Chris's muscled free hand stretched up and over his own shoulder to grasp Jeff's shirt. He plucked the wrestler off of his back like a pesky bug and hurled him across the room—where Jeff crashed against the wall and slid to the floor, looking dazed.

Kelly screamed. Isabel cried in pain. And, at some point during the melee, the clothing in Isabel's hand tumbled to the floor.

As the sweatshirts flopped open, several objects fell to the rough floorboards, skittering to a stop at Kelly's feet. A syringe . . . then a flurry of small, liquid-filled vials and an amber container of pills.

The room fell absolutely still as Kelly stooped to pick them up.

Almost immediately, Chris's thick fingers splayed open, freeing Isabel, and for a moment Kelly felt a flash of sheer terror for her own life as he looked down at the stuff in her hands. Then the big football player faced Nathan.

"I s-swear, man, I didn't tell no one," Nathan stammered, his palms raised in innocence.

"You told!" Chris accused him. "You lousy big-mouth."

"Hey, man. No. Honest." Nathan was backing rapidly toward the bedroom door where Paula stood, silently observing the scene. His eyes darted between his much-needed exit and a seething Chris, judging relative distances.

"I'll kill you, zit!" Chris roared, throwing himself forward.

Nathan dove for the door just as Kelly stepped between the two of them. "Stop it! Stop!" she screamed, stomping her foot and, remarkably, for a moment he did. "Isabel," she asked breathlessly, "Did anyone tell you about Chris's . . . habit?"

"No," she gasped, rubbing her head, still reeling from the unexpected attack.

"Man, you gotta lay off that crap, whatever it is," Nathan rasped nervously. "It's messing with your mind."

"Kelly," Jeff grunted from his spot on the floor, shifting his body gingerly as if it hurt him, "maybe you'd better back off now, before he maims you too."

Chris looked shocked, and some of the anger drained from his face. "Hurt *her?* I wouldn't hurt a girl."

"What do you think you were doing to Isabel?" Kelly demanded, holding her ground. "You practically pulled out all her hair!"

Chris looked down at his hands and at the mass of fine, dark strands wrapped incriminatingly around his fingers.

"Oh, no," he murmured thickly, still gazing pitifully at his fingers as if they were foreign objects. He swung around to face Isabel, giving her a puppyish look. "I'm sorry. Oh, Izzy, I'm really, really sorry. I'm such a bastard!"

She smiled at him forgivingly. "It's all right. It grows back."

Kelly rolled her eyes. Isabel must really be stuck on the hulk. However, there were more important matters at hand now. "What is the syringe for, Chris?" Kelly demanded.

He shuffled his feet, embarrassed. "It's not what you think. Not like I was on coke or heroin or something. I wouldn't touch that stuff. This is like . . . medicine. It just helps me work out, keeps me on top of my game.''

"He's using anabolic steroids," Jeff explained, pulling himself with a groan to his feet. Coach had lectured the team enough times for him to be familiar with their appearance and what they could do to your body and brain.

"Bingo," Nathan whispered. "Now we all know."

Jeff took one of the vials from Kelly's palm. There were three others like it. "Testosterone cypionate," he read the label. "Is this just a five-day supply?"

Chris looked away from him.

Jeff let out a low whistle. "You must be taking one or two hundred milligrams a week." He snatched the amber container and examined it. "More of the same. No wonder you've been flipping out, man! You've been stacking the injections with the oral form."

"I gotta lot riding on this year!" Chris shouted. "I *need* the stuff to compete for the big spots. You think jocks at other schools don't take every advantage they can?"

Jeff shook his head. "That stuff can really screw you up. It's dangerous."

"You could have hurt Isabel," Kelly pointed out. "Not to mention Nathan." *And what about Brian?*

Chris glared at Nathan. Clearly he still bore him considerable resentment. "I wouldn't hurt Izzy," he said distinctly.

"Are these all you have, Chris?" Isabel asked.

He looked down sadly into her wide eyes. Finally he nodded.

"May I keep them for you?"

"I, uh . . . I dunno," he muttered nervously.

She smiled at him encouragingly. "I like you, Chris. I'd like you even if you weren't big. I just don't want to see you get hurt. Please? Just until we get home. Then I want you to see a doctor."

Chris gazed tenderly at her. "All right," he agreed at last, as if wanting to make up for the way he'd mistreated her.

Only then, Kelly wondered if it had been another sort of guilt that had prompted him to relinquish his drug supply so easily. Guilt for what he'd done to Brian.

Kelly held the lantern high. Paula and Isabel walked on either side of her down the path toward the outhouse.

"Where *are* the police?" Isabel muttered.

"Would you knock it off? That's the fourth time you've said that in the last half hour," Paula complained. It was nearly nine o'clock now, and another moonless night.

"What's wrong with you? Don't you *want* the police to come?" demanded Kelly.

Paula looked surprised, then thoughtful. "Of course I want them to come. I just don't think throwing a fit over it will help." She glanced irritably at Isabel.

All afternoon, Paula herself had been a basket case, fretting over Porter leaving them, wondering when he'd show up. But in the last couple of hours she'd grown strangely calm. Kelly wished she could be as patient.

"Maybe he never reached the police," Isabel said slowly, glancing speculatively at Paula.

"What are you talking about?" Kelly asked.

"She means," Paula explained, "whoever attacked Brian got Porter too."

"There's no motive for killing Porter," Kelly pointed out.

"Someone drowned my Brian," Paula said in a shaky voice. "What was the motive for killing him?"

Kelly winced at the harshness of Paula's words. It seemed that by now they all assumed the worst.

"Besides," Paula continued, "a psycho doesn't need a reason to kill. He selects his victims at random. He might be planning to pick us all off, *one at a time.*"

Kelly stopped and closed her eyes, feeling the terror seep through her veins. She seriously considered ordering her bladder into an indefinite holding pattern. Tramping back and forth through the woods to the outhouse—even in groups—didn't seem very wise if there was a bloodthirsty killer lurking nearby.

But she had to admit—Paula's psycho theory did have one psychological advantage—it was easier to believe a stranger had drowned Brian than to accept the possibility that one of the group was a murderer.

"There is one other way Brian might have died. Maybe . . ." Isabel murmured, glancing apologetically at the petite cheerleader. ". . . maybe no one killed him . . . maybe he killed himself."

Paula stared at her for a second before breaking

into hysterical sobs. "How can you say that? How can you even *think* Brian would do a thing like that!" Her voice was shaking, her enormous blue eyes streaming with tears.

"It's not likely Brian would consider suicide," Kelly said, putting an arm around Paula's shoulders and pulling her along the path. "I knew him as well as anyone, and he had everything going for him. He'd been accepted into the academy. His family was well off financially. He had great grades, and even pulled a fourteen hundred on his boards."

"So, why did he sign up for this retreat?" Isabel asked, her voice uncharacteristically sharp. "If his SATs were so hot and he'd already been accepted at the academy, why come at all?"

Kelly glanced at Paula. "Because his girlfriend was here."

"Ah!" Isabel arched a brow cynically. "I remember now. The inseparable pair."

"I think we can rule out suicide," Kelly said firmly. "Come on, let's go pee and get back to the cabin. I'm not crazy about being out here any longer than necessary."

On the way back, Kelly was less occupied with her own discomfort, and the other two girls had stopped bickering. She suddenly became very aware of the woods and the sounds issuing from them. It was as if someone had turned up the volume knob on her senses.

Nearby, almost within reach, she thought she heard a soft crunching sound, echoing the pattern of her steps. Kelly stopped, held up a warning hand. Paula

140

and Isabel halted close behind her. A rustling of leaves, just off the path, also ceased. Kelly slowly raised the lantern.

"What's wrong?" Isabel whispered hoarsely.

The orange light picked out a subtle movement behind a tree, but only Kelly seemed to have seen it, for neither of the other girls said anything.

Someone's out there . . . following us. "Nothing," Kelly murmured, her pulse drumming in her throat. She didn't want to shake up Paula again. "Let's just keep moving."

"Hit me."

Jeff looked uncertainly across the table at Chris. The football player's face was solemn, challenging, still unhealthily bloated since his last flare-up. Or the swelling might have been a side affect of the steroids. The firelight gave his features a demonic quality, exaggerating the deep cleft in the center of his chin—an old scar?—the hollows around his eyes.

"You sure?" Jeff asked.

"Do it," Chris growled.

"All right, but it's your funeral." Jeff dealt him another card, then studied his own hand. A pair of kings—one of them a club—and the queen, jack, and ten of clubs. He could ride on the pair of kings or risk the king of hearts on a chance he'd draw the ace of clubs for a royal flush. He'd never gotten a royal flush before.

"Are you in?" Chris placed a dollar bill on the table.

"Yeah, I'm in. I'll keep this." For some reason Jeff didn't feel lucky today.

"Playing it safe, huh?" Chris asked.

"Yeah."

Behind Jeff, the outside door creaked open. He immediately thought of the police and put down his cards. "Geez, it's about time."

Nathan walked in, alone, shuffling his feet.

Jeff picked up his cards again with a groan. The waiting was even beginning to get to him. For the girls' sake, he'd put on a calm front throughout the evening, but by now he could feel the tension settling in a rock-hard lump at the back of his neck. He needed a diversion to take his mind off of this place. Poker wasn't quite doing it.

"Where's Angel?" he asked. Nathan and his new girlfriend—probably his only one, ever—had ignored Porter's parting command and gone off almost an hour earlier for a walk. Their courage had prompted the remaining ladies to band together for a quick hike to the john. Jeff and Chris offered to escort them, but they'd refused and he hadn't pressed, figuring they needed at least a little privacy.

"Aw," Nathan laughed, "She's off chasing chipmunks again."

"What you let her do that for? You were supposed to keep an eye on her."

"Man, I couldn't help it. She just lit out. I couldn't keep up with her. She's nuts about those things."

Jeff shook his head, slapping down his cards in frustration. "We don't know what's out there! No one should go wandering off alone."

Actually, he preferred to see people in larger groups than two—just in case Brian's killer was in their midst, one of them. He hadn't forgotten about the missing knife. But he figured Nathan and Angel were an even match, weirdness-wise. If anything happened to one of them while they were together, it would be pretty obvious who was to blame.

"You should have stopped her," Jeff said solemnly, checking his watch. Kelly and the other two girls should be along any minute now. "If Angel gets lost and the police show up and we're not all together, we'll have to wait for them to find her."

Chris tapped his cards on the table and coughed politely. "Jeff?"

"Yeah?"

"Do you think they're really coming? It's getting awful late." He sounded like a scared little kid, a complete turnaround from the raging bull of a few hours earlier.

"Of course they're coming," Nathan broke in. "Porter just took longer reaching the main road than he'd expected. Maybe he got lost and had to stop for the night, you know, wait for light. Even a total klutz in these woods will eventually run into a house or a road or something." Nathan sat down beside Jeff and leaned close. His breath smelled of beer. "Know what I think?"

Jeff couldn't help scowling at him. "Would you knock off with the booze! This is serious business."

"Has nothin' to do with my choice of refreshment," Nathan said, waving a dismissive hand.

143

"What I think, deep in my gut—you know how you feel stuff like that? Deep, deep, deep in your gut?"

"You're drunk and incoherent."

"He's right," Chris seconded. "You are definitely trashed."

"Well," Nathan admitted, "maybe a little. But a couple days like these are a good reason to get plastered. You know?"

"We know, Nathan." Jeff leaned to the left to try to avoid his malty breath. "So, what does your gut feel?"

He cast a Chris a condemning look. "My gut rumbles every time I look at *him.*"

"You're probably hungry. Eat something," Jeff suggested. Then, although he hadn't planned to, he continued, "I have to admit my gut's been acting up too. Only it's rumbling, 'Porter . . . Porter . . . Porter.' "

"What are you talking about?" Nathan cried. "You think Porter had something to do with Brian drowning?"

"Think about it," said Jeff. "First the guy gets us out here, alone. Makes sure no one will come looking for us for *five whole days*. No phone. No car. Total isolation."

Chris looked worried. "You serious, man?"

Jeff tilted his head to one side, considering. "It's possible. He hates students, can't wait to get out of the school at the end of the day."

"But that's crazy. Kill all of us?"

"Crazy is the perfect word," Jeff insisted. "Porter is crazy—at least, if he's behind this he must be. And,

144

worst of all, we're at his mercy. He can do anything he wants. We have to play by his rules.''

Jeff shivered as he recalled Porter's words from the day before: *I thoroughly enjoy mind games. . . . Before these five days are through, you'll realize just how seriously I take my games.*

"Hey, this is super rad," Nathan said, letting out a long breath. "Porter claims he's going off for help. Instead, he hikes a couple hundred feet away, then stops. I can see him now, out there, watching us. Waiting for the perfect moment to jump his next victim."

Chris's eyes widened. "Why would he do that?"

"I haven't figured that out . . . yet," Jeff admitted. "And I haven't figured out what we can do to stop him either."

"Then there's only one thing to do—drink my way to the land of forgetfulness." Turning on his heel, Nathan disappeared into the boys' bedroom.

At the same moment, the outside door flew back on its hinges. Kelly, Paula, and Isabel piled through like Keystone cops in an old silent movie.

"Oh, god!" Paula gasped. "Something's out there. It was stalking us!"

Jeff looked at Kelly. She nodded, blowing out the flame on her lantern, while Isabel bolted the door behind them.

"There were definitely footsteps following us," Kelly gasped, automatically scanning the room. "Wait—who isn't here?"

"Angel!" Nathan announced, sweeping out of the

145

back room, a Coors raised in his hand as if in a toast. "Exotic temptress and brave huntress."

"Huh?"

"She's stalking chipmunks," Jeff interpreted.

"She's out there alone?" Isabel asked, looking concerned.

Paula let out a bitter laugh. "I wouldn't worry too much about *her*. She was probably the one trailing us. It would be just like the bitch to try to spook us that way."

Kelly sat down on the bench beside Jeff. She felt safer already, just being near him, even though she still wasn't convinced she should totally trust him. "We don't know that it was her. If she's not back in ten minutes, I think we should send out a search party."

"I agree," Jeff said, looking straight at her.

She couldn't help noticing the intent way he was watching her. Feeling a blush heat up her cheeks, she quickly stood up and moved away. "I'm getting some warmer clothes on, in case we have to go out," she told him.

Kelly walked toward the girls' bedroom. She wished—oh, god, how she wished—Jeff was alone with her in this remote cabin. Truly alone, without this incredible terror surrounding them, jerking at their nerves every other minute, making them afraid to trust each other.

Chapter 9

The day after Thanksgiving, a cold rain began at dawn. Drops spat against the windowpane beside Kelly's cot, waking her. She rolled over, blinking dry eyes. Her perfume bottle lay on its side on the raw wooden sill above her. She reached up, set it on its delicate pedestal again without giving much thought to how it had fallen. The rain was mesmerizing. Droplets lashed out like tiny daggers at the glass, as if trying to cut through to her. But they're only water, she reminded herself. *Water in the air, in the lake. Water, water everywhere.*

Still groggy from sleep, she recalled her middle-school earth science class. The water cycle. Moisture from lakes, streams, and oceans evaporates. Forms vapor in the air, rises to make clouds, eventually becomes too heavy and condenses into droplets, then plummets from the sky as precipitation—rain, sleet, hail, snow.

This might be the same water that drowned Brian, recycled, she thought sadly.

She pressed her hands over her face. The hurt was still unbearable. It weighed her down, tarnishing the way she looked at everything and everyone around her. She'd always trusted people, believed in their basic goodwill. Even her mother's, rationalizing that she must have had an important reason for leaving her family.

But since the horror of Brian's drowning, Kelly just didn't know what to think, or who to trust. She wanted to believe Jeff's story about being obsessed with some girl, jogging instead of resorting to the traditional cold shower he might have taken at home. She desperately longed to keep on believing that Chris was—deep down—a good guy, Isabel was as sweet as she acted, Porter was just a well-meaning but strict teacher, and Nathan was a hopeless, but basically harmless, jerk. She even found herself wishing she could stumble on some piece of evidence that would prove Angel's innocence. When she'd returned to the cabin on her own the night before, the girl had seemed so sad. She looked as if she desperately needed a friend.

Kelly forced herself take a deep breath and open her tear-filled eyes to stare across the room. Paula and Isabel were no longer in their beds. But Angel was still in hers, lying on her side, watching her raptly.

Kelly involuntarily shivered. How long had the girl been lying there, staring at her? "Were you following us last night?" Kelly asked.

Angel looked blankly at her for several minutes. Then, after glancing at the door, she focused on the heavy locket below her chin and whispered, "I was protecting you."

"Protecting us?" Kelly repeated doubtfully.

She thought back to the night of Brian's death. Angel hadn't responded to Paula's cries for help or arrived at the lake with the others. In fact, it was several hours later when she'd finally returned to the cabin. At the time everyone had been too tired and distraught to really question her.

Now the moment had come, and Kelly had to struggle to keep her voice steady. "Where were you when Brian drowned?"

Angel continued to avoid her eyes.

"Please tell me what you know," Kelly begged. "Brian was my friend."

Silence.

Kelly stared at her. The girl was weird, no doubt about that. But that didn't make her any more of a suspect than anyone else. The most brutal killers often turned out to be quite average-looking people. The notorious Hillside Strangler in San Francisco had actually been two men. Two average-looking guys, one of whom was said to be incredibly charming. Reading about that case in sociology had forced her to question her trusting nature.

Kelly lifted her bare legs out of her sleeping bag and moved across cold floor boards to Angel's bed. What secret was Angel keeping so close to her heart?

"Did you find any chipmunks yesterday?" Kelly asked, smiling tentatively.

There was a glimmer of reaction in Angel's dark eyes.

"What are you going to do with them, if you catch any?"

"I *won't* put them in a potion."

Kelly winced at her own cruel cut about calling Angel a witch, coming back to her. "I'm glad. They're sweet, soft creatures. I always think of that

Disney cartoon, you know the one with Donald Duck and the train and—"

"Chip and Dale."

"That's the one," Kelly said, smiling a little more broadly. Now at least they'd established some common ground. "What school do you go to?"

"St. Bartholomew's," Angel pronounced in a monotone.

"Do you like it there?"

Angel sat up in bed, fingered her ugly charm, shrugged. It was the first time in forty-eight hours Kelly hadn't seen her writing in her diary, or at least clutching it.

"School is pretty gross, no matter where you go," Kelly admitted. She decided against asking her about clubs and extracurricular activities. She couldn't see Angel on the pep squad. Debating team was out. And any yearbook committee would have to be pretty desperate to ask her to join.

"I was wondering," Kelly began again, "how did you end up on this retreat?"

"My parents."

"Are they trying to help you get into a tough school or something?"

"Anywhere," Angel said vaguely.

"Your parents . . . want you to leave home?"

"My parents want me to be just like them. *But I'm different!*" Angel stated with emphasis, as if knowing what Kelly had been thinking a second earlier.

"You certainly are that, Angel," she said gently. "But being different isn't necessarily bad. Listen—

150

can you look at *me* and talk, instead of at your medal?''

Angel's gaze obediently rose to meet hers, and the electric emotion in the girl's eyes rocked Kelly. "That's better," she gulped, unable to cover the shake in her voice. She took a moment to compose herself before continuing. "Wednesday night, Thanksgiving eve. You were out in the woods."

Angel nodded. "I'm an insomniac."

"Really? You mean you never sleep at night?"

"I sleep two or three hours most nights," Angel said solemnly.

"That's terrible. I couldn't take that."

Angel tipped her head to one side. "I write in my diary or walk to pass the time."

"Where is your diary?"

Angel blinked as if something sharp had pricked her. "I . . . I'm not sure."

"Did you lose it?"

"I . . . maybe . . . I guess I must have."

Kelly let out an exasperated breath. She was getting nowhere this way and sensed Angel was lying to her. She'd try another angle.

"What did you see that night, Angel? You already told me about Jeff."

The girl lowered her huge dark eyes, yesterday's mascara smudged around them in wide raccoon circles.

"I saw your friend . . . in the boat."

Kelly's stomach knotted. "Jeff?"

"No."

Thank God! "You mean Brian? Was he with someone?"

"Yes."

"You're sure?"

"There were two people in the rowboat," Angel said, pronouncing each word distinctly, as if it was important to her that Kelly understand. "They were talking . . . then shouting."

Kelly swallowed, feeling grateful for Angel's cooperation, although she still hadn't answered half of her questions. At least she'd established that Paula hadn't been mistaken. "Could you see this person clearly enough to identify him?"

Angel hesitated, but at last shook her head. "No. It was dark."

Kelly felt a measure of relief seep into her nerves. Angel had observed Jeff somewhere other than in the boat, which supported his story—running, yearning for some girl's body other than her own. Damn him. Probably Sharon Lewis. She'd overheard Sharon telling a friend backstage that Jeff had brought a friend to the school musical, just to see *her.*

Another thought struck her. "Did you actually see Brian fall into the water? Did this other person push him?"

"It looked like it."

Kelly's heart thumped in her chest. "What did he . . . or she do then?"

"Jumped in after him."

"As if to save him . . . or to push him under?"

Angel considered this for a minute. "I couldn't tell."

"You were right there, Angel." Kelly's voice was thick with frustration and sorrow. "Why didn't you try to save Brian?"

Angel sniffed, a tear rolling out of the corner of one eye. "I—" She shook her head.

"*Why?*" Kelly demanded, her teeth gritted in spite of her resolution to remain patient.

"I can't . . . I can't . . . oh, Kelly, I can't swim!"

And suddenly so much of what had happened two nights before made sense. Terrified yet unable to pull herself away from the tragic scene she was witnessing, Angel had remained close to the edge of the lake, doing the only thing she could think to do at that moment. Scream for help at the top of her lungs.

Through sobs of remorse, Angel told the terrible details. It had been *her* unearthly cries that had awakened Kelly and the others, summoned them to the lakeside. But by then it had been too late for Brian. Realizing he must have drowned as she stood helplessly by, Angel slunk off into the woods to be by herself, too ashamed to join the others. Only hours later, cold and hungry, had she returned to the cabin.

"Did you write all this down in your diary?" Kelly asked.

Angel nodded. "It doesn't matter now. It's gone."

But if it could be found again, Kelly couldn't help thinking, Angel's account might well hold further information helpful to the police.

Kelly thought about telling Jeff, Paula, and the others what she'd learned—that Angel had actually witnessed the murder. But something made her wary of sharing that information. And even though Angel

153

swore she'd told no one else, Kelly couldn't be sure that was true. The girl's grip on reality seemed, at best, fleeting. She decided to keep the information to herself until the police arrived.

If they ever did.

Kelly and Angel stepped out of the bedroom. "Why didn't anyone wake me?" Kelly asked.

Jeff, Nathan, and Chris were seated at the long picnic table in the lounge, playing poker. Paula, wearing the same clothes as the day before, was buttering slices of toast, Isabel stirring a skilletful of scrambled eggs over the fire.

"I didn't see any point," answered Paula. "The police weren't here."

Chris scowled in concentration at his cards. "I still don't get this game. What's better, a pair of something or a row of them?"

"A row?" Jeff choked.

Kelly smiled, in spite of the feeling of foreboding that seemed to sing louder and louder through her nerves. Chris was such a lamb at times.

"I'll help him out," she offered, stepping behind Chris.

"Hey, man," Nathan said. "I don't think you should let her do that."

"Why not?" Chris demanded.

"Haven't you ever heard of cheat teams? All she's got to do now is signal her boyfriend there to let him know what you got."

Chris turned his wide face up to Kelly with an innocent, questioning look.

"You know I wouldn't do that to you, Chris," Kelly said, flashing Nathan a disgusted look.

"Oh, yeah," Nathan taunted. "She's just humoring you. We all know it was you who drowned Brian. What did he do to set off the 'roid rage? Find your cache before I did? Did he threaten to turn you in to your coach?"

Chris's face tightened, the skin flushing beneath its beard-stubbled surface.

"Quit baiting him!" Jeff ordered. Nathan let out a snide laugh. "I'm the only one who sees him for what he is." His eyes narrowed cunningly. "I have an eyewitness account of Brian's last moments alive, and as soon as the police arrive, they're gonna hear it. Then everyone will believe me."

Isabel's hand lightly touched Chris's shoulder, as if to reassure him he was doing well to restrain himself.

Chris stared at Nathan in disbelief. "Don't you remember? You and me . . . we ran down to the lake together. I never left the cabin until then." He looked at Kelly, then Jeff and Paula in turn. "I swear it. I never did."

"Nathan," Isabel said softly, "if Chris says he didn't leave, I believe him."

"I do too," Kelly seconded quickly.

Nathan chuckled to himself. "No skin off my teeth, gang. We'll just let the cops sort out the good guys *from the stark raving lunatic killers!*"

His triumphant shout broke off when Paula knocked the pan of eggs over, burst into tears, and ran from the room, slamming the bedroom door behind her.

"I don't think she can take much more of this," Isabel sighed.

None of us can, Kelly whispered to herself.

"Nathan, why didn't you tell us before that you were down at the lake?" Jeff demanded.

"I didn't say the witness was me," Nathan muttered, looking as if he might have let slip more than he'd intended. "Come on, folks, lighten up! Let's play cards!" He scooped up his hand. "I'll open with a bid of ten big ones. Like Mr. P. always says, I love a good game!" Drawing a wad of paper money out of his jeans pocket, he slapped a ten-dollar bill on the table.

Kelly felt the blood rush into her brain as she stared at the hefty bankroll in Nathan's hand. "Where did you get that much money?" she demanded, grabbing Nathan's hand before he could stuff it back into his pocket.

"None of your business, Red," he retorted. "Come on, guys, let's play some real poker here."

But Kelly's brain was racing. If someone killed a person, wouldn't he naturally try to blame it on someone else? Survival instinct? At first she'd assumed Nathan's obsession with pointing the finger at Chris was just his way of paying him back for humiliating him in front of the others, but now she wasn't sure.

Kelly looked at Jeff and said slowly, "Brian always carried a lot of money on him."

Jeff's eyes narrowed. "And our friend here says he never has more than a couple of dollars on him at a time. Isn't that what you told me, Nathan? Just yesterday?"

"Yeah . . . I guess." Nathan was beginning to look truly worried. "But this is mine, man. I wouldn't be dumb enough to kill a guy for a lousy hundred fifty bucks."

A hundred fifty dollars, Kelly mused morbidly. Two years ago a thirteen-year-old kid from her neighborhood was strangled by a classmate for his Airwalks.

"So, where'd you get it?" Jeff demanded, his voice grating.

"Hey!" Nathan stood up shakily from the table. "No way are you going to turn this around on me. The dough is *mine!*"

"Where?" Jeff persisted, his blue eyes dangerous. "Where did you get it?"

"Work!" Nathan shouted. "Is that okay with you? It's my last paycheck—for two weeks of pouring grease over stale popcorn, sweeping sticky theater floors, tearing thousands of little paper tickets."

"Why didn't you leave the money at home?" Kelly asked. "You knew there wouldn't be any place to spend it here."

Nathan let out a long sigh and shook his head, clamping his mouth shut..

Jeff answered for him. "His father. He's a drunk. He probably would have spent it, if he'd found it."

"Is that right, Nathan?" Isabel asked gently.

"Yeah," he admitted reluctantly. "My old man, he's got the bourbon touch. Anything he touches turns to booze." He gave a bitter cough. "I kept a little in the bank once. He found the passbook and emptied the account."

Chris was apparently not convinced. "Maybe the

police won't believe that story any more than they'll believe the lie about me being down at the lake."

"Guess we'll just have to wait and see," Nathan muttered.

By noon, the rain had changed to a miserable gray sleet that fell thickly from the sky. The clouds were low, bleak, unbroken. Despite the dropping temperature, the sleet melted to a muddy slush as soon as it hit the ground. The lake became invisible from the cabin windows.

The group made a fresh batch of eggs, ate, and washed the dishes.

Kelly's head started to hurt, as much from straining to put all the pieces together in the mystery of Deep Creek Lake as from the dismal weather. "I wish I'd brought aspirin or something."

"I don't have anything either," Isabel apologized.

"Paula?" Kelly asked, rubbing her pounding temples, squeezing her eyes shut for a moment.

"No. No, I didn't bring anything like that."

"You, the walking medicine chest, have nothing? Last time we went on a field trip, you carried three kinds of pain-killer."

"I had my period, all right? So sue me."

Kelly moaned. "My head."

"Maybe if you lie down for a while," Chris suggested.

"I don't think so."

"What about a little fresh air?" Isabel asked. "I'll go with you. We all have cabin fever by now."

"Yes," Kelly decided, taking a deep breath. "That sounds like a good idea."

"I don't think you should go anywhere," Jeff warned.

"I'll go out if I feel like it!" Kelly snapped. "If I don't, I'll go stark raving mad."

Jeff appeared hurt, and Kelly was instantly sorry she'd jumped down his throat. But it was true—she desperately needed some release from the pressure of waiting.

"Maybe we should all pack up and leave together . . . like Jeff said before," Chris murmured. "We could make it to the road by dark."

"*If* we started out in the right direction. Anyone remember which way it is?" Jeff asked. "There must be six different trails leading into our clearing."

"I'm not going out in this weather, even to go to the outhouse," Paula stated. "I don't care if I burst."

"Use an empty can from the trash like I did," Nathan said casually.

"Oh, gross. You didn't!"

"I did." He grinned.

"Where'd you put it?" Paula demanded. "I don't want to kick it over or anything."

"I've *got* to get out of here!" Kelly screeched, rushing for the door. She grabbed her windbreaker from a peg and plunged outside.

The sleet was coming down in sheets, whipping the evergreen branches, making it impossible to see more than a foot ahead as she tugged the nylon jacket over her head and pulled up the hood. The garment really wasn't enough protection. She'd left her heavy winter jacket at home because it took up too much space in her bag. Besides, it made her look like a bright red polar bear.

She'd gone only a few steps into the woods when she heard Isabel calling to her to wait up. Reluctantly, she obeyed, standing with her head turned away from the stinging ice pellets, but it wasn't Isabel who jogged to a halt in front of her.

"You shouldn't be out here alone." Jeff looked worriedly at her, shook the melting sleet out of his dark hair.

"I almost feel safer away from everyone," Kelly confided hesitantly. "I don't know who to trust anymore."

"You trust me, don't you?"

She looked at him earnestly. "I want to."

"I wish you would," he murmured, stepping closer to her, a warm, convincing light in his eyes. The rain didn't seem to be bothering him. All of his attention was focused on her, and she felt flattered that he seemed unaware of the weather. "Why can't you trust me?" he asked.

Kelly felt her heart melt. She shook her head. "So much doesn't make sense. You never even spoke to me at school, totally ignored me on the bus trip up here and all during the afternoon of our lesson with Porter. In fact," she went on, her voice rising accusingly, "you went out of your way to avoid me. Then, as soon as Brian . . ." She gulped, closing her eyes for a second to let the wave of nausea pass. "Well, now you suddenly want to be alone with me."

"I see," he said slowly.

160

Kelly looked up into his blue, blue eyes, needing to understand. "It's as if you want something from me now—something you didn't before. And it seems connected with Brian's death."

He tucked his chin down into the collar of his varsity wrestling jacket, muffling his voice. "It's not that I didn't *want* it before."

"What?" Kelly yipped, not sure she'd heard him right.

"I mean, it's not that I didn't want you before—" He blushed. "Sorry, that sounded crude. I mean, I wanted to get to know you, but I couldn't because being with you drove me crazy. I couldn't concentrate on studying. I *needed* this course, Kelly."

"What about Sharon Lewis?"

"Huh?"

"Never mind." Kelly grinned, feeling slightly delirious. She fluttered her lashes at him. "Being near me was that hard?"

"To put it mildly," Jeff growled playfully. "After Brian drowned and the course was off, there was no reason why I couldn't talk to you. But then you wouldn't give me the time of day—which was understandable because you thought I might have had something to do with your friend drowning."

Kelly's skin glowed with warmth despite the melting sleet soaking through her windbreaker. He liked her. *He really liked her!*

She glanced back toward the cabin. The sleet was coming down so hard it formed an impenetrable gray curtain. No one could see them. When she looked back up into Jeff's eyes, they were the most beautiful liquid color. He raised a hand and wiped the rain from her lashes with his fingertips, then bent slowly over her. She could feel his warmth even before he touched her. Then his arms wrapped around her, pulling her against him.

His kiss was sweeter than any of the hundreds she'd imagined in her most optimistic dreams. Kelly reached up and draped her arms around Jeff's neck. As soon as she sensed him starting to ease away to end it, she pressed her lips firmly against his, letting him know she was perfectly willing to continue this for as long as he liked. Before the night was over she was determined to tell him that she was madly, hopelessly in love with him.

Nathan stepped up behind Angel. "You turn me on something fierce," he growled in her ear—the one from which dangled a black voodoo doll earring.

She continued staring out the window, at the opening of the path Kelly and Jeff had taken minutes earlier.

"Didn't you hear me?" Nathan was accustomed to negative reactions from girls. A slap in the face or fist in the gut he could take—but no response at all? Somehow that was worse. "I said, you're hot. I want you!"

"Jeff and Kelly," Angel murmured.

He threw up his hands. "What have *they* got to do with *my* lust?"

"They're out there, alone."

"No, they aren't alone. They're together—probably doing it in the bushes somewhere . . . which is where we should be right now. It'll take your mind off all this morbid death crap.'' He peered around her shoulder. Her expression hadn't changed. "I have loads of condoms in my suitcase, if that makes any difference.''

"Where's Paula?''

"In her bedroom! And Isabel is over there in the corner, reading. And Chris—the Madman—took off for the bedroom claiming he was going to take a nap, but he's probably shooting up again. Why are you so freakin' interested in everyone else but *me?*''

"It will happen again.''

Nathan sat down on the floor at Angel's feet, wrapped his arms around her tiny ankles, and rested his head against her knees, which were enshrouded in the skirt of her black gown.

"What will happen again?'' he groaned. Four chicks in the woods with no chaperone for miles around. What did it take to get some affection these days? Not that he'd ever been very successful in that area—but, technically, conditions seemed ideal.

Angel let out a worried whisper. He wondered if she sometimes frightened herself as much as she spooked others. He figured she was harmless, all an act. But she sure had the rest of the group fooled.

"Angel,'' he tried again. *"Pleeez,* let's go for a walk. Just a little one. Like Isabel said, the fresh air will do you good.''

"Yessss,'' she cried, "a walk!'' Breaking free from his encircling arms, she ran back into the girls' bedroom, coming out with her long, black, hooded cape.

163

"Perfect for a stroll in a gentle shower," he approved happily.

Isabel looked up with a drowsy yawn from her book. "Where are you two going?"

"Out," Nathan said, taking Angel's cape and flinging it around both their shoulders. "Don't wait up, Mother."

"Stop!" Isabel cried, suddenly alert. "We can't all split up like this. It isn't safe."

"Aw, are we scared?" Nathan teased wickedly. "Well, you've got the hulk behind door number one to protect you. And if he turns on you, you've got Princess Paula behind door number two as a witness. And when they find your bloody body, then maybe everyone will believe what I've been trying to tell you about Chris Baxter!"

"Nathan!" Isabel cried, her eyes pleading. "Don't go out there!"

Ignoring her, he swung the door open and ushered Angel out into the stinging sleet. "She was beginning to piss me off, you know?" he mumbled.

Angel peered out from under the hood that was wide enough for both their heads. "They went this way."

"Who? You still on this Jeff and Kelly kick? Hey, listen, sweet lips, they don't need our company any more than we need theirs. By the way, don't you think red lipstick might be more becoming than black?"

She grabbed his arm and began tugging him into the woods.

"I mean, not that I'm one to complain about a lady's fashion sense," he continued, running to keep up with her, "but I personally find a nice bright red much more luscious. This is far enough, let's stop here, the cabin's out of sight."

Angel dragged frantically on his arm, her eyes wide with fear. "We must find them," she choked out. "They are in danger!"

"All right, all right."

He apparently wasn't moving fast enough to suit Angel. With a muffled cry, she released his arm, ducked out of the cloak, and ran on ahead down the path. Nathan stood alone, dripping hood pulled low over his forehead.

"Great!" he shouted into the storm. "Talk about leadin' a guy on! Well, if you think I need a woman *this* bad, you've got another think coming!" He was disgusted, drenched, and his pants fit accusingly tight in the crotch.

Nathan stared down the path in the direction Angel had disappeared, then back the way they'd come. What the hell was he supposed to do now? If he returned to the cabin without Angel, Isabel would know he'd struck out, yet again. She'd probably tell the others. They'd all have a good laugh at his expense.

On the other hand, the woods were making him edgy now that he was alone. And it was really dark. Suppose he had been wrong about Chris? Suppose there really was some psycho out here, lurking, waiting patiently for his next victim. Or maybe, as Jeff had suspected, that psycho was Porter. The teacher had given in to his request for a reduced rate on the crash SAT course almost too easily. Either he had a soft spot in his heart no one knew about, or he had an ulterior motive.

Nathan undid a button over his chest and touched the knife strapped under his shirt, the leather sheath reassuringly snug against his ribs. He scanned the rough tree trunks and matted tangles of dead briars surrounding him. The sleet came down harder than ever, making visibility even worse. No. He'd better go back to the cabin. But what about Angel? What if someone jumped her?

Jeff had really gotten on his case last time he'd left her out here alone. Nathan had never felt responsible for another person before, and he wasn't sure he liked the job. But he had, after all, talked her into coming out with him.

"Angel?" he cried into the wind as it lashed needles of ice into his face. Her name seemed to fade away only a few feet in front of him, smothered by the roar of the wind and the clatter of little ice pellets hitting dry leaves.

"Angel!" he tried again, as loud as his lungs allowed. A twig snapped directly behind him. He spun around to face a figure standing only a few feet away. "Oh, it's *you!*"

"Hello, Nathan."

"I was just looking for—"

"I see you have the knife."

"The knife? Oh—" Looking down at his chest, he could see where his hand had left an opening in the cape and his unbuttoned shirtfront. A glint of cold silver showed above the beaded buckskin sheath. "I was going to give it back, you know," he said sheep-

166

ishly. "It's just . . . I feel safer with it, until the cops arrive. Know what I mean?" He let out an unsteady laugh, not liking the unswerving look in those eyes.

"It would help if you knew how to use it."

"You know how to throw a knife? Come off it."

"I do. Let me show you."

Nathan looked doubtfully at the hand extended toward him. "This oughta be good," he said with an uneasy chuckle. "Where should I stand?" He handed over the knife.

"Where you are is just fine."

"That big old pine over there would make a good target. Hard to miss. Can you throw that far?"

There was a short pause, and Nathan noticed how the fingers, a moment earlier grasping the leatherbound hilt of the knife in an overhand throwing position, now repositioned themselves so that the razor-sharp blade extended from a fist, firmly held.

"It won't go very far that way," he said. "Let me show you—"

As he'd spoken, reaching out, the knife swung downward in a lightning-bright arc, finding the opening in the cape, piercing his shirt, his flesh, slicing neatly between his ribs. He could feel the icy steel penetrate his organs, the searing pain, sudden weakness in his limbs.

"What—" he croaked. "You?"

"I would have let you live if you'd kept your mouth shut," the voice explained as he fell forward onto his hands and knees. "Good-bye, Nathan." Then footsteps moved slowly away down the path, and he was alone.

He tried to call for help, but found his lungs too weak to push the scream out over his lips. Nathan braced himself on one hand, with the other searched for the hilt protruding from his chest, intending to pull it out. But his reflexes weren't working properly and even when the leather knob bumped repeatedly against his fingers, he couldn't grip it.

The pain! Oh, God, the pain was awful—like a live thing clawing within him! Blood spewed out of the wound, spattering the slushy ground. Jesus, he didn't know he *had* that much in him!

The last thing Nathan remembered came as an instinctive flash through his brain—he must wedge the other arm in front of him when the supporting one gave out. Because, if he fell forward on his chest, the blade would drive straight through him.

Then his face was in the leaves.

Chapter 10

It hadn't seemed to matter that the temperature was hovering around freezing, or that sleet trickled from the night sky between the graceful branches overhead. Kelly felt blissfully warm cuddled in Jeff's arms. For a few minutes, the sadness of having lost Brian slipped into a deeper corner of her mind, where the hurt didn't hurt as badly. She'd found a new friend and her first real love. Jeff.

Then she observed Jeff's shy smile stiffening, his eyes locking onto something behind her, and she spun around to see Angel standing a few feet away.

"We must go back to the cabin. Now!" the girl added urgently when Jeff and Kelly exchanged wistful glances. "It's too risky to stay."

Kelly had looked forward to a slow stroll back to the cabin with Jeff's arm around her. But at Angel's insistence they settled for a brisk jog, holding hands.

At the cabin they counted heads again. One missing.

"Where's Nathan?" Kelly asked.

"He and Angel went out for a walk right after you and Jeff left," Isabel said.

Kelly looked quickly at Jeff, who shrugged. They couldn't really get on Nathan's case for disobeying the rules since she and Jeff had been as guilty. She turned to Angel. "How long ago did you leave him out there?"

"Maybe . . . fifteen minutes?"

"He'll come slinking back after everyone's asleep." Chris chuckled. "So we won't be jiving him for striking out again."

But Kelly noticed again that the mischievous twinkle which seemed to lurk just beneath the surface of Angel's eyes when they'd first met was no longer there.

"We can't wait," Angel said tightly, her eyes bright with fear. "We have to find him!"

Jeff shook his head. "No. We stay here. If Nathan's in danger, then we'll all be placing ourselves in jeopardy by going after him."

Angel rushed at Jeff, clutching the front of his shirt with her long black nails. "We must go now! Now, now, now!"

With a grimace of distaste, Jeff pried her fingers off. "Chill out a while, will you?"

Tears streamed down Angel's face as she staggered backward, despair in her dark eyes.

"Jeff?" Kelly asked, disturbed by Angel's violent reaction. "How about a compromise? If he's not back in an hour, we'll go look for him."

He sighed, not pleased. "All right, if it'll make you feel better."

By eleven o'clock the sleet had turned to rain, then stopped altogether, but Nathan still hadn't returned. Kelly solemnly distributed the three lanterns to Jeff,

Paula, and Chris. She, Isabel, and Angel walked close together within the pool of light.

Not far along the path that Angel indicated she and Nathan had taken, they found a dim shape.

"It's him!" Chris shouted.

He was lying in a puddle of his own blood.

Jeff held out a hand, blocking the path. "On second thought, maybe you girls should go back to the cabin."

"Oh, no, is he—?" Isabel's voice broke off.

Angel dashed forward, knelt beside Nathan with a pitiful shriek. Brushing Jeff aside, Kelly ran to her side.

Blood. The sticky red stuff had leaked everywhere, on the black cloak twisted around Nathan, on his shirt, smeared all over his hands which were curled up near a mud-covered knife on the ground.

Kelly stared at the boy's ghastly white face. He certainly looked dead, but something compelled her to press her fingertips to his beard-stubbled throat. "There's a pulse!" she cried hoarsely.

"Oh—th-thank God—" stammered Paula. "He's alive."

"Not for long, from the looks of him," Jeff said grimly. "He must have lost gallons of blood."

But, miraculously, or perhaps simply because the cloak had knotted up beneath him, pressing against the severed blood vessels, the flow seemed to have clotted—so maybe there was a chance.

Dear God, please, help him! Kelly prayed silently. *Help us all!*

Jeff picked up a large leaf and used it to retrieve

the knife from the mud. He started to slip the blade into his jacket pocket.

"Wait!" Chris said in a gruff voice. "Let's see what the bastard stuck him with."

Caked with dried blood, the weapon was almost unrecognizable.

"That's *my* knife!" Isabel gasped, reaching out for it.

Chris stepped between Isabel and Jeff's hand, his eyes a clear deep color Kelly had rarely seen. "I don't think any of us should mess with it."

"He's right," Jeff said, carefully sliding the knife into his pocket. "The police will need to determine if there are prints on it."

"But it's mine!" Isabel insisted.

Jeff glared coldly are her. "Maybe that's why *you* should be the *last* one to have it."

With a sinking heart Kelly looked at the soft-spoken Indian-American girl. He was right. Whether or not the knife had been stolen, once it resurfaced Isabel would know best how to use the weapon.

"But the knife . . . someone took it . . ." Isabel insisted, a bewildered look on her face. "Oh, I never would have brought it if I'd thought—" Her hand flew to her mouth.

"Thought what?" Jeff demanded.

She stared straight ahead, avoiding everyone's eyes. "We should get Nathan back to the cabin," she muttered dully.

Jeff scowled at her. "If you didn't stab Nathan, who did?"

Isabel glanced sadly at Angel, then at Paula—the

two girls whose boyfriends had been viciously attacked over Thanksgiving vacation. "I thought I knew . . . about Brian," she whispered. "I was just waiting for the police."

"What do you mean—you thought you knew?" Paula glared at her furiously. "If you *knew* who killed Brian, why didn't you say so in the beginning?"

Isabel choked on a throatful of tears. "It was . . . just so . . . so very sad . . ."

It was as if Paula, who still hadn't gotten up enough energy to change her clothing since the morning Brian drowned, received a jolt from a high-voltage wire. She ran at Isabel, screaming. "What are you talking about, you Indian slut? If you know, say something!"

Isabel opened her mouth hesitantly. Before she could get out another word, Paula slapped her across the face, then fell on top of her in a frenzy.

"Stop her!" Kelly shouted.

"You tried to steal him from me!" Paula screeched as Jeff and Chris dragged her, kicking, off a terrified Isabel. "I saw the way you looked at him! He's mine!"

He was *yours*, Kelly's brain amended. *Now he belongs to Gweemush.*

Feeling sick at the returning image of Brian's bloated body lying at the bottom of the lake, Kelly whispered hoarsely, "This can wait. Isabel's right, we have to take Nathan back to the cabin."

"Just a minute," Jeff said in a voice that sounded calm and strong even now. "Isabel, if you know what happened to either of the boys, you should say so." He clamped a strong hand around Paula's arm when

173

she looked as if she was going lunge for the other girl again.

Sitting limply in the mud, Isabel stared down into her lap. "I really believed I understood what had happened. But the pain the truth would cause—" She shook her head. "I'd decided to keep it to myself."

"That's crazy! You don't ignore a murder like a bad quiz score," Kelly scolded.

Isabel looked at her blankly.

"You don't sound so sure of your decision anymore," Chris said, as he reached down and gently lifted the Indian girl to her feet.

"I'm not. The fact someone tried to kill Nathan changes everything. I mean, I didn't *see* anything that night at the lake. I was in the cabin—but I knew. At least I thought I knew because I'd overheard—" She waved the thought away. "But I must have been wrong. Whoever tried to kill Nathan must have killed Brian too."

"Not necessarily," Kelly said.

Everyone looked at her.

"What do you mean? There are two psychos on the loose?" Jeff demanded.

"Maybe," Kelly murmured thoughtfully.

No one slept that night. The cabin stank with the smell of dried blood, and once in a while Nathan surfaced to semi-consciousness long enough to groan or utter a few incoherent words. Sitting on the floor near his cot, Kelly prayed he'd stay deep enough under to be unaware of the pain.

There hadn't been much they could do for him. The

first aid kit Porter had brought contained only a tiny bottle of Mercurochrome, a few pinky-sized Band-Aids, and some mosquito repellant—like they'd need it in November. *This is worse than trying to plug a torpedo hole in a battleship with a paper towel!* Kelly thought in frustration. Paula finally advised them to simply cover the wound with a couple of layers of clean sheet. Then all they could do was keep him warm and pray he hung in until Sunday . . . and hope like hell the bus would arrive as scheduled.

Angel curled up on the cot beside Nathan like a protective cat. Her face was drawn but almost pretty in its paleness. She'd scrubbed off her makeup, and, although she still wore black and her hair could only be tamed a certain amount with a brush, she looked almost normal. It was as if the character she'd played no longer appealed to her. Had she gone too far, only realizing it too late? Kelly wondered.

The rest of the group crashed in the lounge, waiting for daybreak. The cabin was filled with tense silence, each of them thinking the same thing. Who would be the next victim?

As Kelly waited out the endless hours of darkness, her head throbbed from lack of sleep and the strain of trying to make some sense of what was happening to them. One of her classmates was dead, another close to it, and their teacher was missing. She agonized over details of the past few days. At the foggy edges of her mind, a clue lingered she couldn't quite wrap her mind around. But she knew if she could, she'd very likely discover Brian's killer.

"You all right?"

Kelly glanced up to see Jeff standing over her. "Yeah."

It was three o'clock in the morning. He looked exhausted, with deep purplish circles under his eyes. She wondered if he blamed himself for what had happened to Nathan. If Jeff had stayed at the cabin, he might have insisted Nathan and Angel stay too. But then Kelly would have been out there alone. Maybe *she* would have been the victim. She shivered at the thought of cold steel tearing through her flesh.

Jeff studied Kelly's expression. "What are you thinking?"

She drew a shaky breath. "Nathan must have pulled the knife out after his attacker left him for dead. Can you imagine having to do that? Even splinters make me squeamish."

"Try not to think about it. Listen, at least we have one factor in our favor."

"What's that?"

"Tomorrow is Saturday. If we just make it through the next thirty-six hours, we'll be alive to get on the bus and go home."

"I was just thinking about that," she murmured, smiling at him softly. "I've never wanted to be in my own house more than right now."

Jeff put an arm around her and gently stroked her cheek, but something inside of her refused to be comforted by his tenderness. Or maybe the warning came from outside—the wind whistling through the trees, whispering—whatever evil had driven a knife into Nathan and pulled Brian under Deep Creek's chill waters was searching for its next victim, and the bus wouldn't

176

come for them on Sunday . . . would *never* come for them . . . And she'd just found out Jeff liked her, maybe as much as she liked him . . . *Damn, what lousy timing!*

I don't want to die! she thought, the horror swelling inside of her until it was almost unbearable. *I don't want Jeff to die. I don't want any more of my friends to die!*

Except for an early-morning mass outhouse break, everyone stayed in the cabin all day. No one felt like eating breakfast. However, later that afternoon, Paula and Isabel insisted that what was left of the group take some nourishment to keep up their strength, so they made peanut butter and jelly sandwiches. Only Angel refused food and insisted on staying with Nathan, although he slept soundly now.

PB&Js, Kelly recalled fondly, biting into the sweet, gooey-thick sandwich. That's what she'd called them when she was a little girl. Would she ever have a little girl of her own to make sandwiches for?

She glanced toward the window. The wind had died, and the temperature seemed milder. A fog rose off the lake, creeping up the wooded hill toward the little cabin.

It's Gweemush, Kelly thought irrationally, *reaching out to get us because we won't come down to his water kingdom.* The same water that killed Brian. The water that must have streamed down Nathan's face, contorting in agony as Isabel's knife plunged between his ribs. The water rose up off the lake in a fine mist— coming for them.

177

Jeff moved over to sit beside her on the couch and stayed there, his arm around her shoulders as if he'd sensed her need for him to be near.

"It'll be all right," he whispered, as if to reassure himself as much as her. "The bus will be here tomorrow at noon, and we'll all go home."

And I'll never find out who killed my best friend. Even if the police mounted a full-scale investigation, Kelly couldn't believe there would be much to work with. Any tracks that might have been left around the lake when Brian drowned were undoubtedly obliterated by the students' amateurish search, or washed away by the storm. And after days in the water, what would Brian's poor bloated body tell? If they ever found it.

"Tell me what you're thinking?" Jeff asked.

Maybe the only way to find Brian's killer is to do it now . . . before the police come. "Nothing," she whispered, and gave him a quick kiss on the cheek.

Suddenly, staying alive and keeping her friends alive, Kelly's only goal for the past few days, took a lower priority. It wasn't that she no longer cared if someone tried to kill her, or succeeded. It was more a matter of calculated risk. If she were careful, *very* careful—she might be able to use the element of the dwindling time left before the bus came to her advantage.

Why did you leave me? Kelly would probably never be able to ask her mother or Brian that question. But she had a chance to find out why her friend had to die—if she was clever enough.

Jeff squeezed her hand and touched his lips to her

hair, just above her ear. "I'd better go check on Nathan. Be right back."

Kelly nodded, sitting up straight, watching Jeff's strong shoulders disappear into the boys' bedroom. Wearily she glanced around the lounge in the waning light. Paula was curled up, dozing on the couch. Chris was playing solitaire with Nathan's deck of cards. He had all four aces out. Methodically he counted out three cards from his hand, turned them over, checked for places to play them, counted out three more. She hadn't seen him actually move a card or play one from his hand in almost an hour. Isabel sat beside him on the bench, her head resting on crossed arms.

Kelly got up from the couch and ambled over to the window. The fog was so thick she could barely make out the shape of the big pines closest to the cabin. From the corner of one eye, she glimpsed Jeff's jacket, hanging on a peg beside the door. Without thinking about what she was doing, she sidled over and reached into its pocket and slowly took out Isabel's knife. It must be a key piece to the puzzle. But where did it fit?

As she stood holding the knife, she remembered isolated events: her perfume bottle knocked over; black curls in a fire, started for what reason? To destroy something? Could that something have been Angel's diary? Kelly recalled the fear in Angel's eyes whenever she tried to make her talk about the night Brian drowned. And Isabel's obvious reluctance to divulge a secret she was convinced could only hurt someone.

So much that had started out as a mystery was falling into place in Kelly's mind—like a row of dominoes set on end and given a little push. Only sometimes the spaces between the dominoes were too wide, and one failed to knock the next down. She still had to fill in the gaps.

Hearing Jeff's footsteps creaking across the room next door, Kelly hastily looked around, assuring herself that no one in the lounge had seen her take the knife. She hid it behind her back and sat down again.

"How's Nathan?" she asked, almost too brightly, when Jeff reappeared.

"Still out cold. I think he's running a fever, though. He's sweating like crazy."

Kelly frowned. "Infection from the wound?"

"Maybe. Or shock. Angel tucked a couple more blankets over him." He paused, sitting beside her, and it was tempting to melt in his arms, blank everything from her mind except Jeff and the dreamy way it felt to be with him. But she couldn't let herself do that—not yet.

Kelly took a deep breath and remarked in a clear voice even Angel would be able to hear from the bedroom, "I think I know who killed Bri."

Across the room, Chris's cards stopped flickering on the tabletop.

"You *know?*" Jeff asked, frowning.

"Yes, but I can't tell you who it is just now. There are a few . . . a few things I have to go outside and get . . ." she murmured vaguely, ". . . to make sure they're still here for the police."

Jeff stared at her in horror as she stood up. "You can't go out there alone!"

180

If he came with her, it would ruin everything. But she hadn't expected him to willingly let her leave the cabin.

"All right," she said lightly. As Kelly stood, she shielded the knife beside her body. Then in a voice low enough so that only he could hear, she said, "Of course you can come, but we'll be hiking pretty far into the woods, away from the lake. Just let me get a dry jacket." She went into the girls' room, located her thickest hooded sweatshirt in her suitcase, and pulled it over her head. Scooping the mini-corder out from beneath her bed, she snapped a blank tape into it. Then she slid it, along with Isabel's knife, into the hand warmer sewn on the front of the sweatshirt. With a last heart-tugging glance toward the lounge where Jeff waited for her, she pushed open the window over her bed and climbed through. She'd had to lie to him, in case he tried to follow her. She needed to buy time. As she jogged down the path toward the lake, she was more afraid than she'd ever been in her entire life.

Paula's head felt fuzzy, although she hadn't really slept, only drifted in and out of consciousness, still aware of conversations around her. She'd also heard Kelly go into the bedroom and, a few minutes later, Jeff started pounding on the door, calling Kelly's name. Eventually, he'd let out a curse and slammed out through the front door.

Suddenly Paula was fully alert, panic rippling through her veins. She had to stop them! Didn't Kelly know how dangerous it was, talking like that about Brian's murderer? But before Paula could decide exactly what to do, the outside door opened and closed a second time.

She rolled over. Isabel and Chris had left too. She was alone in the cabin, with only Nathan—unconscious in the other room—and Angel.

As if alarmed by the disturbance in the lounge, Angel poked her head out of the bedroom. Paula looked at the girl and actually laughed out loud. She was such a ridiculous person—a nonperson really.

Angel's head jerked around as if she hadn't realized Paula was still there. "Don't touch me!" she rasped out.

"Why on God's green earth would I want to do that, you freak?"

Angel shook her head, every muscle tense. "No reason."

"You know," Paula said slowly, "if I believed that you and Brian ever—"

"I didn't mean we'd really met," Angel explained quickly. "He just . . . he seemed nice. I imagined if I were different, we might have been friends."

"That's what you meant by meeting in another life?"

Angel nodded, glancing nervously over her shoulder, into the bedroom.

"What did you *really* see at the lake the night Brian drowned? What did you see you didn't put in that stupid diary?"

Angel's eyes narrowed. "*You* took my diary."

"So what?"

"What did you do with it?"

"I burned it. It was full of lies. Lies about Brian.

I couldn't let you show that stupid book around. Just think how that would have hurt him! Now—" Paula glared at her. "What else did you see?"

Angel clamped her mouth shut and shook her head stubbornly.

"Does that mean you saw nothing, or you won't tell me?" Slowly Angel began backing into the bedroom. Paula stood up and took a step toward her. "Or maybe you're saving your lies for the police, is that it?"

Angel slammed the door in Paula's face. Then Paula heard the sound of a bed being dragged across the floor, bumping against the door.

She moved forward until her lips touched the rough wood panels. "If you ever say anything bad about my Brian," Paula screamed, "I'll kill you! I'll stalk you down and *kill* you, you freak!"

Isabel had taken Chris's hand and led him out of the cabin because she hadn't wanted Paula or Angel to hear what she had to say. Something had been troubling her since the day of the bus ride to Deep Creek Lake. Isabel had been eavesdropping, which she knew was wrong, but at the time she'd rationalized it as a way of getting to know people. And fitting in at her new school had been important to her. She'd signed up for the special SAT class over Thanksgiving vacation because some of the most popular students at Thomaston were rumored to be taking it.

However, almost from the beginning, the trip had taken a wrong turn. And now she could no longer keep what she'd heard on the bus to herself. Chris had trusted her to hold his steroid supply; she believed she could trust him too.

Isabel led him just outside the clearing, behind a wide-trunked maple, and gazed up at him. His dark, strong features made her think of an African god.

"I have a confession,' she said softly.

"What, Izzy?"

"I hope you don't hate me, after you hear what I have to say."

He looked troubled and shocked. "You didn't—"

"No!" she gasped. "Of course not. I had nothing to do with Brian's death or what happened to Nathan. But I must tell you this, in case anything happens to me."

He frowned. "No one would hurt you. You're so beautiful and kind.

She grinned at his compliment, but went on quickly before she lost her nerve. "I overheard Paula and Brian talking on the bus, on our way here. They were discussing a version of the Indian tale I told at the campfire, our first night at Deep Creek. They'd heard a simpler version of it in a freshman American history class."

"But they said they didn't know it."

"No. They said they didn't know any ghost stories. But this wasn't a ghost story—it was a love story."

"Love story?" Chris repeated. "But everyone *died* in it!"

"Exactly. Everyone died."

Isabel watched his expression change through several emotions before she continued. "Paula thought the story she'd heard was romantic—the young lovers vowing to remain together no matter what. She didn't realize that it was just as important to them to be with their families and friends as it was to be together. She equated the Indian lovers with herself and Brian. She was obsessed with the idea of a *suicide pact*. At least, that's what I believe.''

Chris considered her theory for a moment. ''I don't think Brian would do that, kill himself.''

''He didn't want to. He was arguing with Paula, trying to convince her they shouldn't do it.''

''That must be why he came up here, to talk her out of her idea,'' Chris mused.

''Right. And probably to make sure Paula didn't hurt herself while she was away from him. But she wasn't listening. On the bus while Kelly was napping, I had my eyes closed and must have looked asleep too. Paula accused Brian of not loving her, because he wouldn't make the final sacrifice for her—his life.''

''That's nuts!''

''You said it.'' Isabel fixed Chris with a meaningful stare.

''Wait—are you saying he killed himself for the bitch?''

Isabel shook her head slowly. ''No, I don't believe Brian ever intended to do that. Somehow, his plan to talk her out of suicide must have gone wrong . . . there was an accident . . . or something.'' She shook her head, wishing she understood all the details.

''That still doesn't explain the stranger in the boat—or Nathan,'' Chris pointed out.

''No,'' Isabel admitted with a sigh. ''There are a lot of unanswered questions.''

"I wouldn't put it past Nathan to have drowned Brian for his money." Chris's eyes lit up. "And if Paula discovered the truth, she might have tried to kill Nathan in revenge!"

Sadly, Isabel gazed up at Chris. "I've thought the same thing. It makes a tragic sort of sense. Nathan might have taken the knife and kept it on him for protection. You know, he really was terrified of you."

"Gee. I didn't like him, but I wouldn't have—"

"I know." Isabel reached up and hugged him, hard. She was going to shape him up. Get him off the steroids and work on his self-esteem so that he'd never need to depend upon chemicals to prove his worth again.

"What about Porter?" Chris asked. "How does he fit into all this?"

"That's another thing I don't know. I can't figure why he stranded us out here."

Chris frowned, wrapping his big arms protectively around her. "I don't think we should wait until tomorrow to see if the bus shows."

"Why not?"

"Just a feeling." He looked down at her. "How about a hike through the woods?"

Chapter 11

Kelly had less of a plan than she'd have liked. The best arrangement would have involved a police detective and a half dozen sharpshooters lurking behind trees, keeping her covered. As it was, all she had for insurance was Isabel's knife, tucked snugly into the pouch over her stomach. She'd have to be careful how she used it, though. She didn't want to end up like Nathan.

Poor Nathan. He'd been looking for proof—but not the truth. That mistake might have cost him his life. He'd trusted the wrong person.

And the others? Chris, who so desperately longed to play college football but had fallen prey to a drug habit with violent side effects. Jeff—darling, sexy Jeff with his dazzling blue eyes and wonderful warm lips, and . . . everything else. Isabel and Paula and Angel—her three roommates, as different as three girls could possibly be. Yet each had her secrets and had been, she was certain now, maneuvering behind her back.

As she made her way down to the lake, Kelly thought back to a moment earlier when she'd slipped through the bedroom window. She'd had to move her perfume bottle aside to avoid knocking it over. Wasn't it lying on its side or repositioned slightly several times when she'd returned to the room? She wished she'd taken closer note of the time. That damned window could have been a revolving door for all the action it had seen in the last few days.

Kelly pulled her sweatshirt close around her ribs, shivering. Night had fallen early again, and she felt as if she could almost touch the heavy darkness closing in around her. Only the fragile silver crescent moon provided any light. But it was enough to see the uneven ground beneath her feet, which was fortunate because she hadn't been able to take a lantern. A few stars even peeked out from behind the last wisps of low clouds, trailing after the storm. It would be a clear, beautiful winter night.

The last night of my life? Kelly wondered.

She ran along the beach to the boat house, threw open its wobbly door, and started to drag the little rowboat out. The curved hull made a loud grating noise against the pebbles, and every few seconds Kelly's nerves prickled and she stopped to listen for the sound of following footsteps.

Ironically, out in the middle of the lake where Brian had drowned was where she'd be safest, and where she'd gather the proof she needed to catch Brian's killer. From there, in the moonlight, she could see anyone stepping out from behind encircling trees. And sound traveled remarkably well across the water, unlike in the woods.

Her plan was simple. From her position in the rowboat, she would ask her questions. Her guest—who should be arriving any minutes—would provide the answers, unaware that she was recording them for the police. She wasn't sure of the legal technicalities of using a taped conversation in court. But the tape should at least convince the police to take Kelly's hunches seriously.

There still were no footsteps. She hoped her quarry would show up soon, but not just yet. Oh, God, please not until she'd rowed at least twenty feet into the lake! She began dragging the boat toward the water again.

The scraping of the hull against the coarse grains of brown sand, the hushed lapping of the waves, and her strained breathing were the only sounds. Again, Kelly stopped to catch her breath. Then she heard them. Running steps. Sliding across the slick pebbles at a rapid clip.

Frantically, Kelly gave the little boat's stern a hard push. The bow lifted in the shallow water. Another push and she could feel the boat become buoyant. She had one foot over the side, ready to climb in, when a movement caught her eye. She froze, sensing it was already too late to run, too late to bother rowing. For a second, she shut her eyes, then backed out of the boat and forced herself to turn around.

"Hi, Paula," she said, the air escaping her lungs in a long whoosh.

"What are you doing?"

So much for plans.

"I was just about to row out for a little ways, to clear my head." Kelly hoped her voice sounded steady. She could no longer tell. "I think I know how Brian died."

"So you said. But you couldn't, you weren't here."

Kelly shook her head. "I didn't need to be here. When it comes down to it, only one answer is really possible."

Paula looked confused. "The stranger. You've found him?"

"There is no stranger. Never was a stranger."

"There wasn't?" Paula asked.

"This place is just as deserted as Porter promised in his brochure. He intended it to be this way from the start. No distractions. No interruptions. Remember?"

"Mr. Porter killed Brian!" Paula gasped, her face contorting, as if physically trying to absorb the impact of the statement. She twisted around as if expecting to see the history teacher spring out of the woods at her.

Kelly could believe, at least at that moment, that Paula might have accepted any explanation. Any but the awful truth.

"No, Paula," Kelly whispered hoarsely, *"He* didn't kill Bri. What did you do to Porter? Where is he?"

Paula flashed her an angry glare. "How the hell should I know where he is? First you claim Porter's to blame for Brian's death, that he schemed it from the start. Then you say you don't know where he is, like some terrible thing happened to him or he's still stumbling around in the woods, totally lost." She pouted. "I don't think you have any idea what's been going on."

"I wish I didn't," Kelly murmured over an egg-sized lump in her throat. Tears burned her eyes. "I wish I didn't need to know or tell anyone about it, ever. Nothing will bring Brian back, and I suppose his death hurt you as much as it did me. But I can't let you go free, because of what you did later, to Nathan.''

For a moment Paula just stared at her in disbelief. She laughed. "You think *I* killed Brian?''

"And you tried to kill Nathan. And possibly Porter too.''

"You stupid bitch! I *loved* Brian. I'd never do anything to hurt him!'' Tears glistened in Paula's lovely china-blue eyes.

"Yes,'' Kelly said softly, shifting her right hand almost unnoticeably toward her hand warmer, then into it. She moved her foot against the gravel to mask the sound of the recorder button clicking on. "I believe you must have loved him in your own way. You don't care about much else in the world, do you, Paula? Little animals, creatures you can control, that will love you back, blindly. That kind of devotion is what you always need. And even Brian wouldn't give you that. As much as he loved you, he wouldn't follow you blindly. He wouldn't *die* for you, Paula.''

Paula, the beast . . . the wolf, thought Kelly.

The blonde cheerleader let out a dry, hacking laugh. "You're insane! What are you talking about . . . wouldn't die for me? Brian *is* dead. He drowned, Kelly.''

"But not willingly, the way you wanted. Was it as romantic as you'd thought it would be, Paula? The two of you, alone in the night, holding hands as you drifted out across legend-enshrouded Deep Creek Lake. You'd both already loaded your pockets with

191

pebbles from the beach. The weight of the rocks combined with the wet burden of your clothing was calculated to drag you down to the bottom in seconds. Unconditional togetherness. No competition from Brian's parents, from the air force, even from his best friend.''

"You!" Paula hissed accusingly, swiping at the tears trailing her cheeks, stepping toward Kelly although the boat separated them. "He talked about you. How close he felt to you, how you grew up together before I even met him."

"We were friends, Paula. I never loved Brian in any other way, and I'm sure he never thought of me in romantic terms."

Paula shook her head sadly, sagging forward at the shoulders, the heels of her hands braced against the splintery hull of the rowboat. "It doesn't matter. He listened to you. He did what you said but he argued with me."

As prepared as Kelly had been for the wildest rationalization Paula might fling at her, she now stood in shock, her mouth open. *This* was what Paula viewed as competition: someone Brian listened to? Finally she regained enough of her composure to continue, because she *had* to go on and fill in the last few gaps of logic. Only when the picture was complete would the police believe her story, and put Paula away where she couldn't hurt anyone else.

"The only girl Brian ever loved was you, Paula. But you asked for more," Kelly prompted gently.

Paula straightened up, her moist eyes glowing. "I

told him about the legend of the lake. I told him we would be together, forever.''

"You'd be *dead. Dead is dead—whether or not there's another kind of life after this one!*" Kelly shouted. Her head was pounding, mouth dry. This was insane! "It wasn't time for either of you to go. Brian had a future, an exciting lifetime that he looked forward to. And you had one too, dammit!''

Paula shook her head, the pupils of her eyes shrinking, growing distant. She moved along the edge of the boat, closing the distance between her and Kelly. "It was a hobby for me . . . the animals. I tried to love them, to care. I thought if I learned to feel something for them I didn't feel for people, it would prove I was a good person. Kelly, I've never felt a thing for anyone but myself.''

Not even when you drove a hunting knife through Nathan's chest?

In spite of her resolve to stand firm, to not run away until she was sure she had gotten the whole story taped, Kelly took a step backward. She remembered how good Paula was at cheerleaders' leaps, and the girl was getting much too close. But at least they still had the boat between them. Kelly slipped her hand into the handwarming pocket and wrapped her fingers around the hilt of Isabel's knife, wondering if she could actually kill another human being, even in self-defense.

A bitter taste flooded Kelly's mouth, and her stomach heaved, as if she was going to throw up. "Why didn't you drown too, Paula? Did you change your mind at the last minute, after Brian gave in to you and threw himself into the lake?''

''No!'' Paula moaned miserably. ''He *never* gave in. He never really did what I asked. He lied to me, said he'd do it, and I believed him.''

''But as soon as he said it, and the suicide pact became real, it no longer seemed quite as romantic?'' Kelly guessed.

Paula nodded. ''As we walked down to the lake I was happy, because by going with me he was saying: I love you enough to end my life. But once we were in the boat he got weird. He talked about how it would feel when I tried to breathe, underwater. How the cold water would fill my lungs, and the pain. I hadn't thought about pain.''

In Paula's warped mind, death had been beautiful, a soft sleep with a pretty, endless love song playing in the background.

''What happened then?'' Kelly asked.

''Brian stood up in the boat. He told me to stand up with him, but suddenly I couldn't do it. I felt the rocks in my sweater pockets and I could imagine how deep the water was and it was all so . . . so real.''

''That's what he'd wanted, Paula!'' Kelly croaked. ''He wanted to make it real to you!''

''Brian reached for me.'' Paula sobbed jaggedly. ''He was going to throw me in, and I was terrified! I told him no. I told him I'd changed my mind, or at least I was trying to tell him that, but he wouldn't listen. I pushed him away from me.''

Kelly's throat was so dry and knotted she could

194

hardly get out the words. "He fell overboard. It was an accident."

"Yes. An accident. He fell in." Paula looked eagerly at Kelly. "You have to believe that, Kelly. I never meant to hurt him. He went down fast, but I tried to save him. I emptied the rocks out of my pockets into the bottom of the boat and dove in. But—oh, God—he'd gone down so fast. I actually touched him once and grabbed his jacket sleeve, but he fought me and I lost my grip and never could find him again."

"There were no rocks in the boat when I went back to search it the next morning." But Kelly had felt them there against her spine that night. Lumps.

Paula sighed, nevertheless managing a pleased smile. "I got rid of them after Jeff swam out and pulled the boat to shore with you in it. I would have dumped the pebbles sooner, but I'd heard someone shouting for help—Angel, I suppose—so I knew people would be coming soon. While everyone was fussing over you, I made a mad dash for the rowboat . . . like I was going to try a last-ditch effort to find Brian. I pushed down hard on one side of the boat, as if climbing in, and the boat flipped over, dumping the pebbles."

Paula rattled on. Once started, she seemed incapable of stopping herself. "Afterwards, I couldn't think straight. I only knew that Brian would never want people to believe he'd killed himself." She looked earnestly at Kelly. "He said that once—when we were arguing about suicide. He said he didn't want little kids thinking you could just bail out when life

195

got rough. So I had to protect his secret, didn't I? It was the least I could do for him.''

''No!'' Kelly snapped, out of patience with the girl. ''I don't think you cared about Brian's reputation or his wishes. Your motive was selfish. If his parents or yours ever found out that the idea had been yours . . . if your friends discovered what really happened, you were afraid they'd never forgive you. You wouldn't have a friend left in Thomaston.''

Kelly glared at the other girl. There was more and, as awful as it was, she had to get it all on tape.

''Nathan found out,'' Kelly prompted, encouraged by the vibrations of the tape recorder against the knuckles of her right hand, letting her know it was working.

''Yes. He read Angel's diary before I could get hold of it. She'd been wandering around in the woods that night, and saw Brian and me in the boat. I knew if I could just get the diary away from her, chances were no one would believe anything she said—even if they managed to understand it. She was so far out!''

''But hearing the same story from two people might be different.''

''Right.'' Paula sighed. ''People probably wouldn't take Nathan all that seriously either, but if he corroborated Angel's account by digging up additional evidence—even though he intended to put Chris away with it, I knew it would end up pointing to me. Nathan was really beginning to piss me off.''

Kelly shook her head. ''If only you hadn't stabbed him,'' she said. No one could *really* blame you for Brian's death. It really was an accident. But Nathan—

you tried to kill him. That's attempted murder. The police . . .''

A movement in the bushes above the slope of the beach distracted Kelly momentarily. She had only turned her head a fraction of an inch when Paula leaped with incredible agility straight over the boat, at her. She didn't have time to yank the knife from her jacket front before Paula fell on her in a whirlwind of fury, tearing at her face with her nails, yanking her hair.

The plastic recorder case, sandwiched between the rocky beach and Kelly's stomach, knocked the wind out of her. Dizzy from lack of oxygen, Kelly kicked out with one foot, catching Paula hard in the shin.

''Ouch—damn you!'' The girl's grip loosened on Kelly's hair for a second, and Kelly gave her a fierce shove and rolled clear.

But as she scrambled to her knees, the mini-corder slid out of her sweatshirt, and the knife flew out of her hand, skittering across the beach.

''Oh, no!'' Kelly cried.

Unable to reach for both at the same time, she made a crucial choice. Without the knife, she couldn't defend herself. But without the tape, she had no proof of Paula's guilt. She threw herself on top of the recorder.

As Kelly started to push herself up off the ground, holding the mini-corder, she sensed action behind her. Tensing, she braced herself for the tackle Paula was undoubtedly preparing to throw at the back of her knees, determined to hold onto her evidence. However, the blow never came. Feeling a teensy bit triumphant, Kelly started to whirl in the direction of the knife, when she glanced up to see Paula standing over her, a boulder raised in both hands above her head.

Gee, the observation flashed through her brain, *that certainly is a big rock!*

Which was Kelly's final thought before the stone plummeted down with vicious force, connecting with the top of her head, breaking through the flesh and cracking against the bone beneath, and Kelly collapsed in a helpless heap at the feet of a madwoman.

Angel sat in the bushes, her knees pulled up to her chin, rocking, keening softly. She'd come looking for Kelly, to warn her—but had been too late.

Right from the beginning, Angel had liked Kelly. Although the bouncy redhead never really went out of her way to befriend her, she'd shown signs of caring what Angel thought and felt. And if Angel ever decided to be "normal," she'd want to be like Kelly. Popular, with lots of friends. A singer and dancer, competitive swimmer, pretty. Maybe then, normal wouldn't be so bad.

Unfortunately she'd arrived at the last row of pine trees after Paula found Kelly on the beach.

"We'll just wait here and see what happens," she whispered to the metal skull dangling around her neck when Kelly made no move to elude Paula. At first Kelly seemed to be handling the situation all right. The two girls were talking and, although Angel couldn't hear the words, nothing violent was happening.

She was just about to back away to a safer distance

when Paula flew at Kelly in a rage so shocking Angel could do nothing but stare in astonishment. She remembered the look on her mother's face, the mean snarl, snapping mouth, and cutting words when sixth-grader Angel had used Lady Clairol shampoo-in color to tint her mousy brown hair a beautiful shiny black. Her father had beaten her with his belt and called her a slut and told her she wasn't going to grow up to be like *her* mother, a teenage whore who'd had to give up her baby for adoption.

That was how she'd learned Lenore and Robert weren't really her parents. Then they'd scrubbed her head for two hours straight with strong soap, rinsing over and over with scalding water, to get all the color out.

The very next day, while she was still sore with red welts across her back and bottom, she went into Lenore's sewing room, took fabric shears, and cut off the bottom eight inches of her hair, leaving only a ragged stubble across the crown. Then she used the permanent dye she'd bought at Dart Drug on her way home from school a few minutes earlier. And she stopped talking to Lenore and Robert.

All she'd wanted was to be a little bit different, special. Just enough to matter. She hadn't even known what a whore was! But it sounded like an ugly, hateful word, and now, sitting in the cold bushes, Paula's fury reminded her so much of Lenore's that she couldn't make herself move. It wasn't until seconds later when Kelly fell under the weight of a boulder dropped by Paula, her head oozing a red stream, that Angel knew she had to do *something*.

But the idea of rushing Paula terrified her, because now she was armed.

Thrusting Isabel's knife into her belt, Paula picked up the tape recorder that had fallen from Kelly's hands, placed it on a flat stone. With the blood-spattered boulder, she smashed the little machine—once, twice, three times—then threw its remains into the lake.

Gazing with horror at Kelly sprawled on the ground, her brilliant orange-red hair matted with a darker stain, her skin growing almost translucent under the moon's glow, Angel had moved in a crouch, away from the lake. And now she sat and cried for the friend she could have had, if only she'd had the courage.

The woods felt less quiet than at other times. There were subtle vibrations among the trees that might have been sounds, voices, animals scurrying among leaves, falling tree limbs, any number of things. But Jeff couldn't tell one from another.

He'd stopped calling Kelly's name, knowing by now she'd either intentionally given him the slip or was incapable of answering him. He hoped like hell it wasn't the second. After scouring the woods for nearly a quarter of a mile to the north, east, and west of the cabin, he headed straight down the main path for the lake because that was the only place he hadn't searched.

Only a few feet along, he ran into Angel streaking through the woods in the other direction. The look on her terror-pinched face turned his veins to ice. His eyes narrowed. "What have you done to Kelly?" he demanded.

"No! Oh, no!" Angel cried, her eyes wild, enormous. "Paula hit her. She isn't moving . . . I don't know if she's hurt or . . ." Her voice choked off in a sob, and she fell to her knees.

"You don't know what?" Jeff demanded, grabbing her by the elbows and shaking her. But it was no use, the girl was hysterical. What the hell was she talking about . . . Paula *hit* her? "Where is Kelly?"

Angel pointed.

Jeff sprinted off in the direction of the lake, his heart thudding, pulse racing hot. He felt the cold fill corners of his lungs that seemed untouched by air ever before, even in a race. Piercing tiny capillaries with icy stings, bringing him a desperately needed surge of adrenaline.

He skidded down the embankment onto the narrow strip of coarse sand in record time, staggered to an unsteady halt, breathing hard, staring around him. "Kelly!" he shouted with what little air he had left. "Kelly!"

If she was conscious . . . if she was *alive* she must be able to hear him from this close.

"She was right here," a tiny voice said just behind him.

He whipped around. Angel stood, shivering, gazing up at him with petrified eyes.

"You better not be messing around!" Jeff warned her. "Was she here or not?"

"She was!"

"But you said she was . . . hurt." Not *dead*. He couldn't even form the word with his fear-numbed lips.

Angel flung herself down on the damp brown sand in the moonlight. She crawled on her hands and knees, scrambling around like a big black crab, her gown trailing behind her.

She grunted. "Here!" Grabbing Jeff's arm, she pulled him down beside her. "Look, blood! Oh," she moaned, "so much blood in the sand."

Jeff touched the dark spot, still wet, thick and sticky. Around the stain, the sand was pock-marked with footprints and deep gouges, as if a thousand feet—or just four, in a life-and-death struggle?—had scuffed the coarse grains and pebbles into miniature valleys and mountains.

Jeff's stomach lurched. He felt light-headed with fear.

Then he noticed one especially wide, deep rut, the kind a child might have made by dragging a very large, full pail across the sand. Or it could have been formed by the dead weight of a body being dragged.

His heart hammering against the inside of his chest, Jeff took off across the beach, following the drops of fresh blood, praying he wasn't too late.

Chapter 12

Somebody was scrubbing Kelly's back with sandpaper—scratch, scratch, scratch—as if trying to smooth down her shoulder blades and ass to make them even with the small of her back. A rushing sound filled her ears, her mouth tasted like burnt rubber, and her head pounded, getting worse every time the gigantic sheet of sandpaper moved.

Or she moved.

Yes, that was it! *She* was scraping across the rough surface, lying on her back, yet Kelly was doing nothing to make herself move. Therefore, someone was dragging her, by the heels.

Kelly wished she could open her painfully dry lips and tell the idiot in charge, down at her feet, to quit it. All she wanted to do was go back to sleep on the beach beside the lake. But it was cold here, too cold to sleep. What was worse, it was growing very damp, downright wet really. Kelly could feel water lapping at her hair, her ears, and, finally, leaping up in an enormous splash as her legs fell into it.

Her mild irritation with the person who'd disturbed her nap was replaced by a nagging doubt. Should she be more concerned with her surroundings? Her head spun and ached ferociously, making it almost impossible to think or order her body into action. It was all she could do to pry open one eye a crack.

Paula was crouched over her, loading handfuls of pebbles into the front of Kelly's sweatshirt. When she finished, she removed her cheerleader's sweater, tied its long, woolen sleeves around Kelly's throat, and began filling its large patch pockets with more rocks. Heavy black and lead-gray rocks.

Enough to sink a goddamn battleship! Kelly thought through a wave of panic.

"No!" Kelly croaked, her voice barely audible to her own ears.

Paula looked at her, startled momentarily, before her thin lips lifted in a confident smile.

I must really look like crap, Kelly decided.

"It won't hurt for long," Paula promised. She sounded like a nurse reassuring her jumpy patient before giving an injection. In the moonlight her eyes were dilated, huge and shining like flat jet-colored buttons. They had a wild, obsessed glaze.

Kelly shivered with horror and something warm trickled down her forehead, into her eyes. Shakily, she lifted one hand to clear her vision. Her fingers came away dripping with deep red blood.

Kelly thought deliriously: *I'm bleeding like crazy. Maybe sharks will be attracted and they'll polish me off quick. No, there are no sharks in lakes, stupid.* "Paula . . . don't!" she rasped, clawing weakly at the cheerleader with her bloody hand.

"It'll be over soon. Shut up." Paula evaded her outstretched fingers. She started dragging Kelly again by the heels of her soggy tennis shoes, with greater difficulty this time because of the added weight, deeper into the lake where the bottom became soft and silty.

Kelly no longer had the strength to hold up even one arm, let alone fight Paula off.

The water crept in cold swells up along the sides of Kelly's face, carrying with it a reviving power. It lapped up over her arms, which dangled loosely at her sides until they floated, and suddenly her inability to speak became uncontrolled chatter—her only defense against Paula's madness.

"You're burying me with Brian. That's so nice."

"Huh?" grunted Paula.

"With sweet, sweet Brian. I loved him so much. It's only right we'll be together."

Paula stopped and turned to observe Kelly, who was lying on her back in the mucky water. "You're delirious. I'm not burying you *with* him."

"Together," sighed Kelly dizzily, sounding almost happy with the situation.

"Not together!" Paula insisted, tears springing to her eyes. She stamped her foot in the water, splashing both of them. *"We* were supposed to be together, he and I . . . not you and—"

"No mat-ter." Kelly's voice slurred as another wave of throbbing pain blazed through her skull, nearly shoving her over the precipice to unconsciousness. "Cops will . . . will find him. Find me."

"The lake's too deep."

Kelly giggled. *How had she managed that?* "Ah, but good old Brian's parents are very, very rich. They'll spare no expense . . . drag the lake . . . send down divers . . . call in the Coast Guard . . . the merchant marine . . . the ASPCA . . . the—''

"So what?"

"So—" Another bolt of excruciating pain. Kelly squeezed her eyes shut, battling its paralyzing power over her brain. "So they'll find this goddamn sweater . . . wrapped around me, full of rocks. *Your* cheering sweater? Any chance its has your initials inside?''

A troubled look entered Paula's eyes and immediately she stooped down and began untying the arms knotted at Kelly's throat.

Kelly smiled weakly.

"Quit looking so smug," Paula growled. "There's still enough weight to—"

"Rrrkks," Kelly mumbled, her mouth contorting in a spasm.

"What?"

Kelly took a shuddering breath. It was so hard to keep talking when all her brain wanted to do was sleep, let the nightmare end. "R-O-C-K-S! You told everyone . . . stranger attacked Brian . . . in boat . . . you on shore. Police will want to know . . . why Brian has *rocks* in his pockets. *Was he going to throw them at the guy?*''

Paula scowled, absorbing the fact that none of her explanations to the other students would make any sense if Brian's body was found. Everyone would know she had lied. Her eyes flickered indecisively.

Now! Kelly's brain urged. *Do it now before she comes up with another plan!*

Kelly used the precious ounce of strength she'd stored up during the last few minutes to slowly lift her left hand. Inch by inch, she moved it toward Paula's belt, toward Isabel's knife. Just as her fingertips brushed the hilt, Paula's glance dropped, her eyes widening.

"Hey!" she shouted, grabbing for the knife at the same time Kelly's fingers closed around it and pulled it free.

Kelly slashed the air, unable to aim, only wanting to keep Paula away from her. The blade nicked the girl's cheek, opening an angry gash.

Screaming, Paula fell back on her ass in the water, clutching at her injured face. "You little bitch!"

Somehow Kelly rolled onto her stomach and started belly-crawling back through the cold shallows toward dry sand, still clutching the knife in her hand.

"Stop!' Paula commanded, launching herself out of the water.

Kelly twisted around, tears of pain flowing down her cheeks, diluting the fresh blood that had started seeping again from her scalp. She lashed out with the knife, this time catching the shoulder of Paula's T-shirt, and with it some of the flesh beneath. Like an injured animal, Paula screamed in rage, knocking the knife from Kelly's weakening grip with a clenched fist.

For a moment, they just looked at each other, breathing raggedly.

Slowly, a victorious grin spread across Paula's lips. "It's over now, Kelly. You're hurt too bad to fight me any longer."

She was right Kelly knew, and knew, too, that Paula had to kill her to keep her secret.

Paula easily rolled Kelly over onto her stomach. She sat on her back, grabbed two fistfuls of red hair, and forced Kelly's face down into the water, into the rich coffee-colored silt.

I'm going to die. Oh, God, there's nothing else to do. Kelly choked, coughed. Cold mud oozed up into her throat. Her head felt as if it had a fiery core, burning inside like a volcano about to erupt. And the mud filled her nose and throat. And the blackness of death enveloped her in its endless cold.

Suddenly the pressure of Paula's hands left her head and the weight on her back disappeared. Someone pulled her face above water, thumping her on the back so that she could cough dirty water out of her lungs.

There was a struggle, some scuffling nearby, but that was over long before she caught her breath. "Is she all right?" Jeff's voice called out.

"*Are* you all right?" It was Angel, still supporting her so she wouldn't go under again. "Oh, geez, you look terrible."

"Thanks," Kelly mumbled with a lopsided smile, and promptly passed out.

Brian Lopez's funeral was on the morning of the twenty-ninth of November, one week after he drowned in Deep Creek Lake. Police divers had found his body, weighed down by several pounds of rocks in the pockets of his varsity jacket. Officially, his death was listed as a suicide—although Kelly and the SAT group knew better.

During the graveside service at St. Michael's Cemetery, Kelly sat in Jeff's 'Vette, watching Brian's parents as they stood despondently over their son's casket. They'd been joined by only a few close family members. The Lopezes had barred Brian's classmates, including Kelly, from attending the funeral. Mr. and Mrs. Lopez refused to believe that only Paula had been involved—they thought that the others had known and kept the young couple's tragic plans to themselves.

So it was only later, after the priest and family members left the cemetery, that Kelly and Jeff walked down the grassy slope to pay their final respects. Kelly bent over the casket and laid a single red rose on it. For a long while, she knelt, mourning her old friend as Jeff stood silently by.

When she finally looked up through tear-filled eyes, Isabel, Chris, and Angel stood in a circle around the grave.

"We had to come," Isabel said softly.

Chris blinked, looking as if he was close to crying himself. *He really is a sweet boy,* Kelly thought, giving him a dim smile. He bent down and placed a bouquet of autumn-colored chrysanthemums on Brian's casket.

Angel stepped forward. Holding out her hands, she sifted fragrant rose petals through her fingertips. They fell like pink rain over the mahogany lid. "Good-bye, Brian," she whispered. "I would have liked to know you better."

For a while the five kids were silent. It was the first time they'd all been together since they'd left Deep Creek.

"I never had a chance to thank you, Chris," Kelly began awkwardly.

"For what?" he asked.

"Taking off through the woods with Isabel to find help."

Thanks to Chris, the police had arrived a couple hours after Jeff and Angel had rescued Kelly and tied up Paula to keep her from harming anyone else. Chris had decided to see if he and Isabel could find the highway on their own. But before they'd hiked a mile from the cabin, they came upon a half-starved, semi-frozen Alexander Porter. The teacher had stumbled and broken his leg a few days earlier—by catching his toe in one of the natural caverns about which he'd warned his students.

"You know," Chris said thoughtfully, "I'm glad we're all here together. There are some things about last week I still don't understand."

"Like what?" Kelly asked.

"Well, when Isabel and I found Porter, the marker had been removed, and the cavern opening was camouflaged with pine branches. I figure Paula must have slipped out the girls' bedroom window while Isabel was reading in the lounge and the rest of us were searching for Brian. But how did Paula know Porter would walk over that particular spot?"

Kelly took a deep breath to calm herself. Even now it was difficult to talk about those terrifying days. "I asked the police the same question when they took my statement at the hospital. The lieutenant in charge said they'd discovered that half a dozen markers had been removed from trip holes along the route between the cabin and the main road.''

''Paula apparently wasn't taking any chances,'' Jeff commented dryly.

Kelly turned to Angel. ''How's Nathan doing?'' she asked. Kelly had to stay only one night at the hospital, for observation. But Nathan would be there a while longer: he'd had surgery for his knife wound the day after he was admitted. Porter had his leg set and put in a cast. He'd refused to stay even one night in the hospital.

''Nathan's doing better,'' Angel said, smiling. ''He's off the critical list now. The doctors say he might be able to go home in another week.''

''That's great,'' said Jeff.

''I'd like to stop by,'' Kelly added, ''but his nurse said he wasn't accepting visitors, although one of my neighbors who works in his ward told me you'd been over several times.''

Angel smiled. ''He's still pretty shaken by his experience at the lake,'' she apologized. ''Don't take it personally.''

''Imagine what he thinks of all of us,'' Chris said solemnly. ''I scared him half to death and Paula nearly finished the job.'' He shook his head.

Isabel reached up and wrapped her arm comfortingly around the football player's wide shoulders. ''Well, you made up for your mistakes,'' she murmured, then turned to Kelly. ''You should have seen him when we finally reached the highway. For ten minutes or more there were no cars at all, then a big, shiny BMW whipped around the corner. Chris stepped right out in the middle of the road and waved him down. He was so brave!'' She squeezed him.

Chris looked embarrassed. ''I think the guy was afraid of totaling his car if he hit me.'' He hesitated. ''One more question—what about Paula's stranger?''

Kelly shook her head. ''I was never absolutely sure about him myself. But the possibility she'd invented a convenient intruder began to make sense as time went on and none of us spotted anyone in the area. Also, Paula was the only person who we knew was on the scene when Brian drowned. At first, her confusion over the details of what actually happened seemed natural, due to shock. But then I began to wonder if she might be trying to cover something up. Was she protecting someone in the group by claiming a stranger was to blame? Was she protecting herself?''

''But what first tipped you off?'' Angel asked. ''I mean, I actually saw Brian and Paula in the boat and knew no one else was involved in the accident. But you had nothing to go on.''

''That's not exactly true,'' Kelly said. ''Right after Brian drowned, Paula mumbled something incoherent about her and Brian sneaking off, to glide out over the lake in the moonlight. But there was no moon that night, none at all because it was a new moon.''

''She was recalling the scene on Deep Creek from Isabel's story of the Susquehana massacre, the night the Indian lovers drowned,'' Jeff guessed.

''Almost right. Remember, she was inside the cabin on kitchen duty when Isabel told her story. Actually,

Paula was recalling the legend she'd read in history class.''

"I didn't catch that at all," Jeff murmured, shaking his head and looking disappointed in himself.

"I might not have either," Kelly replied, "except for other things you couldn't possibly have known. Each one, on its own, might have meant nothing, but together they were suspicious. For instance, Paula packed only what she'd need for one day, because she wasn't planning on hanging around for the whole course.''

"Oh, I remember you asking her for aspirin," Isabel said.

"She expected to be beyond pain," Jeff observed in a soft voice.

"And then we return to Isabel's very unusual ghost story." Kelly looked at the other girl.

Isabel gave her a half smile. "I had to add on the spirits in the mist to make it qualify as a spooky story.''

"When you told it, I thought it seemed an odd one for you to choose, even if it was about the local area. You were trying to scare Brian, weren't you?''

Isabel nodded. "But Paula was the one who should have heard it.''

"She was so messed up by that time, I doubt it would have done any good," Kelly assured her.

Chris frowned. "But when we found Nathan in the woods after Paula had stabbed him, why did she insist in front of everybody that Isabel tell what she knew about Brian's death? She'd nearly killed Nathan to cover up the facts.''

"I can answer that one," Jeff said solemnly. "If you remember, Isabel was no longer sure that Brian's drowning had anything to do with Paula's suicide pact."

Isabel nodded. "Stabbing Nathan didn't seem to fit."

"And Paula wasn't sure herself how much Isabel knew," Kelly continued. "She got Isabel talking just enough to assure herself that Isabel was only guessing what might have happened. Then when Isabel started to say something more that might have incriminated her, Paula slapped her."

"After that, I was afraid to trust anyone," Isabel said. "After all, I was new at Thomaston. I figured if any of you were at fault, you'd cover for each other."

Kelly sighed. "I wish you'd known us better then. You'd have realized that nothing was more important to me than finding Brian's killer. I'd have protected you from Paula."

"Me too," Chris added with feeling.

"And me?" Angel said softly. "Would you have protected me from her?" Angel had toned down her dark, dramatic look quite a bit since her days at the lake, and now wore jeans and a leather jacket in place of her flowing black gown.

"And you too, of course," Kelly said, touching Angel lightly on the arm. "After what you'd seen Thanksgiving eve, you must have been terribly upset."

Angel took a deep breath. "I was. And when Paula and I went off alone to the outhouse . . ."

"You arranged that on purpose, didn't you?" Jeff asked, a touch of admiration in his voice.

Angel nodded. "I wanted to talk to Paula alone. I had gotten out of my seat on the bus and walked down the aisle to catch one of my frogs—"

"Must have been while I was asleep," Kelly said.

"Yes. And I heard Paula say something to Brian about there being enough rocks at the lake. Well, there isn't a whole lot you can use rocks for at a lake except . . ." Angel blinked, thinking. "Well, I don't know what. But I'd read a biography of the writer Virginia Woolf. That's how she killed herself."

"So you tried to talk Paula out of it."

Angel nodded. "She threatened to kill me if I interfered. I believed her."

Isabel reached out and touched Kelly's sleeve. "Do you suppose there was something more any of us . . . *I* could have done—you know, to stop them?"

Kelly looked at her hands. "No. Brian undoubtedly thought he was doing the right thing by dealing with Paula's obsession on his own. I think he loved her so much, he never would have believed she was as crazy as she was. And nothing would have stopped Paula."

"Brian almost succeeded," Jeff said. "At the very end, he scared her out of doing it, but it was too late for him. That's the real tragedy."

Kelly nodded and her eyes threatened to fill up again, but she made herself keep talking. "There was one other thing that only I knew about," she murmured. "The pebbles at the bottom of the rowboat."

"The ones from Paula's pockets?" Jeff guessed.

"Yeah. I felt them when I climbed into the boat

after I'd failed to find Brian. They stuck in my mind, the feeling of them against my back. I didn't connect the lumps with pebbles from the beach until much later. In the meantime, though, I kept thinking of Brian at the bottom of the lake, *always at the bottom,* never floating as a body would probably do.''

''Your subconscious must have put two and two together.''

Kelly nodded. And perhaps she hadn't wanted to believe what the facts were trying to tell her. She hadn't wanted to believe the terrible scene at Deep Creek Lake her mind envisioned. She hadn't even wanted to believe that Brian, the nicest boy she'd ever known, was dead.

Kelly touched the smooth, gray marble slab. She blinked, and a single tear trailed saltily into her mouth.

''Oh, Bri,'' she whispered. ''If only you'd told me . . . told someone.''

Jeff moved up closer and slipped a strong arm around her. ''You all right?''

''Yeah.'' She took a deep breath. ''I wonder what will happen at Paula's trial.'' Because of the uncertainty of what actually happened that night at the lake, she wasn't being tried for Brian's death. But she'd have to face two charges of attempted murder for what she'd done to Nathan and Kelly.

Kelly thought that the trial was bound to be an ordeal, and her expression must have reflected her distaste.

''I'll be right there beside you,'' Jeff murmured in her ear.

216

She looked up at him gratefully. He'd read her mind. He seemed to be doing that a lot lately. And she *loved* it.

"I know," Kelly said, her green eyes sparkling as she thought of something else she liked about their relationship.

He kissed her tenderly on the lips.

NICOLE DAVIDSON grew up in New England and now lives in Columbia, Maryland, with her daughter and son, two dogs and one cat. Her hobbies include baking (especially desserts!) for her friends and family, working out with weights, and competitive ballroom dancing. Having traveled and lived in a number of cities in the United States and Europe, she enjoys using these exciting settings for the backgrounds of the numerous novels she has written for readers of all ages. Her books for teenagers are often inspired by the real teens in a local high school, where she frequently spends time disguised as a mild-mannered substitute teacher.